12.50

P9-EDU-356

Children
of My Heart

Gabrielle Roy

Children of My Heart

Translated by Alan Brown

McClelland and Stewart

Ces enfants de ma vie
original edition
© copyright, Ottawa, 1977:
Editions internationales Alain Stanké Ltée

Children of My Heart
translation by Alan Brown
copyright © 1979 by McClelland and Stewart Limited

The Canadian Publishers
McClelland and Stewart Limited
25 Hollinger Road, Toronto M4B 3G2

Printed and bound in Canada

Canadian Cataloguing in Publication Data

Roy, Gabrielle, 1909-
  [Ces enfants de ma vie.   English]
  Children of my heart

Translation of Ces enfants de ma vie.

ISBN 0-7710-7838-2

I. Title.   II. Title: Ces enfants de ma vie.
English.

PS8535.0826C4813   C843'.5'4   C78-001611-4
PQ3919.R74C4813

This translation was completed with the
assistance of the Canada Council.

Books by Gabrielle Roy

The Cashier
Children of My Heart
Enchanted Summer
Garden in the Wind
The Hidden Mountain
The Road Past Altamont
Street of Riches
The Tin Flute
Where Nests the Water Hen
Windflower

Part I

When I think back, as I often do these days, to my years as a young teacher in a city school for boys, the first picture that comes, emotion-charged as ever, is that of the opening morning. I had the class of the very smallest. It was their first step into an unknown world. Added to the fear they all felt was the dismay, in the case of some of my little immigrants, at being spoken to in a language that to them was foreign.

Very early that morning I was assailed by the sound of a child's screams amplified by high ceilings and resonant walls. I went over to my classroom door. From the other end of the corridor a heavily built woman was sailing toward me like a battleship, dragging by the hand a small, howling boy. Tiny as he was beside her, he managed at times to dig in his heels and, pulling with all his might, to slow their advance for a second. Then she would take a firmer grip, lift him off the floor and carry him for a further gain. And she had to laugh at how hard he was to manoeuvre despite the odds. They made it to the classroom door where I was waiting and trying to keep a straight face.

The mother, in a thick Flemish accent, introduced her

son, Roger Verhaegen, five and a half, a good little boy, very quiet and docile when he chose – eh, Roger? – while she tried with a jerk to make him stop crying. I had already had some experience with mothers and children, and I wondered if she, for all her muscle, were not one of those who unload on others her own lack of authority, with the daily threat, "Just you wait, you, till you go to school. They'll settle your hash."

I offered Roger a red apple. He turned it down only to snatch it from me a second later when I was looking elsewhere. Little Flemish boys didn't usually take long to tame – no doubt because after the terrifying accounts they had heard, school turned out to be a treat. And in fact Roger soon let me take his hand and lead him to his desk, his cries reduced to subdued sniffles.

Next came George, a silent, expressionless little fellow, led by an aloof mother who gave me the necessary details and went off without even smiling at her son, already seated at his desk. He himself showed little more emotion than she had, and I made a mental note to keep an eye on him – he might well be one that would keep me on my toes.

Then I was suddenly surrounded by a whole group of mothers and children. One child kept moaning with small, suppressed cries. His dreary lament made its way to Roger, who was less consoled than I had thought. He started sobbing again in accompaniment to the new arrival. Others who had been quiet until then took up the refrain. It was in this dreary clamour that I had to go through with their registration. And other children kept arriving and, finding themselves in a place of tears, started to blubber.

It was surely heaven that came to my aid by sending me, just then, the merriest little boy in the world. He came in, hopping and skipping, ran to a desk of his own choice, spread out his new scribblers, and laughing as if at a shared joke, looked up toward his mother, who was watching him in a flutter of happiness.

10

"My little Arthur's not one to give you the least bit of trouble," she said. "If you knew how long he's been dying to go to school!"

This little boy's high spirits were already having their effect. Children around him, surprised to see him so happy, were wiping their faces on their sleeves and starting to look on the classroom with different eyes.

Alas, I lost ground again with Renald, whose mother came in pushing him from behind, overwhelming him with precepts and good advice: "You come to school to get an education. . . . If you don't have an education you'll get nowhere in the world. . . . Blow your nose. . . . Don't lose your handkerchief. . . . Nor all those other things I had to buy. . . ."

This one was weeping as if for a misfortune that stretched from one end of life to the other, and his classmates, without having the least notion of the nature of his trouble, wept with him out of sympathy, all except my little Arthur who came and tugged at my sleeve:

"They're crazy, eh?"

A little later, with thirty-five children registered and more or less settled down, I began to breathe again, hoping for an end to the nightmare and thinking: The worst is over now. I saw little faces, to which I still was unable to put a name, sending me a first, furtive smile or, in passing, a caressing look. I said to myself: We're going to be friends.

And then, from the corridor, came a fresh cry of anguish. My class, which I thought I had won over to confidence, was overtaken by a shudder. With trembling lips they stared toward the doorway. Then there appeared a young father and clinging to him a little boy, the living image of him, with the same dark, grieving eyes and such a stricken look that one might have been tempted to smile if those two had not expressed in equal degrees the very pain of separation.

The little boy, glued to his father's side, turned up at him a face flooded by tears. In their Italian tongue he was begging him, it seemed to me, for the love of heaven not to leave him!

Almost as upset himself, the father tried to reassure his son. He ran his hand through the boy's hair, dried his eyes, fondled him, soothed him with tender words repeated over and over, seeming to say: "It'll be all right. . . . You'll see. . . . It's a nice school. . . . Benito, Benito. . . ." he insisted. But the child kept up his desperate appeal: "La casa! La casa!"

Now I recognized him: an immigrant from the Abruzzi who had recently come to our town. As yet unable to find work in his own trade of upholsterer, he was doing odd jobs here and there. This was why I had seen him one day in our neighbourhood, digging up a patch of ground. I remembered that his little son had been with him, trying to help, that the two never stopped talking as they worked, no doubt spurring each other on, and that this murmur in a foreign tongue, at our fields' edge, had seemed to have a special charm.

I went over to them with the very best smile I could muster. As I came near, the child cried out in terror and clung even more desperately to his father, who trembled on contact. I could see that he wouldn't be much help. On the contrary, with his caresses and soft words he did nothing but keep alive the hope that he might weaken. And in fact the father began to plead with me. Since the boy was so unhappy, wouldn't it be better to take him home just this once, and try again this afternoon or tomorrow morning, when he'd have had time to explain what a school was.

I saw them hanging on my decision, and took my courage in my two hands: "No, when you have to make the break it doesn't help to wait."

The father lowered his eyes, obliged to admit I was right. Even between the two of us we had trouble detaching the child; as soon as we loosened the grip of one hand it slipped away to grasp another handful of the father's clothing. The odd thing was that while he continued to cling to his father he was furious with him for taking my side, and through his tears and hiccups was calling him a heartless wretch, or words to that effect.

Finally the father was free for a moment, while I was holding on to the boy for dear life. I made a sign to the father to disappear as quickly as he could. He went out the door. I closed it behind him. He opened it again a crack to tell me, glancing at the child:

"That's Vincento!"

I let him know the details could wait, for Vincento had almost escaped. I grabbed him in the nick of time and closed the door again. He rushed at it, straining to reach the knob. He wasn't screaming or crying now: all his energy was bent to getting out of that place. The father was still there, trying to see through the glass top panel how Vincento was making out and whether I was able to cope. From his anxious face you'd have said he was unsure how he wanted these events to turn out. And again the child was on the point of making his getaway under my very eyes, having succeeded in grasping the doorknob. I turned the key in the lock and put it in my pocket.

A deafening silence followed, seeming to extend to the father whose breathing I could no longer hear, but whose eyes, wide with surprise, followed our every move.

For the moment Vincento was thinking, his immense eyes taking in the situation. Suddenly, too fast for me to see him coming, he attacked, directing a volley of kicks at my legs. I saw stars but didn't let on. Then the father, perhaps a little ashamed of his son, or on the other hand reassured that he could take care of himself, decided at last to leave.

Vincento, left to his own devices, seemed to be searching desperately for a plan of attack, a strategy; but then, as he

13

really had nowhere to go, he heaved a great sigh, his courage left him, he surrendered. Nothing remained but a little broken creature, with no support, no friend, in a foreign world. He ran to a corner and threw himself on the floor, his head buried in his hands, curled up and moaning like a little lost dog.

At least this profound and genuine distress made my whimperers stop short. It was in the midst of total silence that Vincento sobbed out his lament. Some children, trying to catch my eye, put on a shocked expression as if to tell me: What a way to behave! Others, pensive, contemplated the little shape lying crushed on the floor, and they too sighed.

It was high time to create a diversion. I opened a box of coloured chalk and passed it around, inviting each child to come to the board and draw his own home. The ones who at first didn't understand what I was saying caught on as soon as they saw their companions drawing squares with holes for the doors and windows. They began joyfully doing the same, and to judge by their conception (egalitarian in the extreme) you'd have said they all lived in the same house.

At the top of the blackboard I drew a building that was no more nor less than their houses put end to end and on top of each other. The children recognized their school and began to laugh with the pleasure of locating themselves. Now I drew a path going down from the school to the lower board where the houses were. My jolly little man was the first to have the idea of putting himself on the road, in the form of a stick surmounted by a circle, with eyes on the sides of the head as in certain insects. Then they all wanted to be on the road. Soon it was covered with small people going to school or leaving it. I wrote each one's name in a balloon above the drawings. My class was delighted. Roger, who had come to school in a farmer's straw hat, worked hard to put a cap on the stick that represented him.

14

He ended up with the curious spectacle of an enormous ball proceeding on tiny bits of legs. Roger began to laugh as hard as he had cried at first. A kind of happiness had begun to possess my class.

I glanced at Vincento. His moans were fewer and farther between. Not daring to uncover his face, he tried between the slits of his fingers to follow what was going on, and it seemed to astonish him mightily. Surprised for a moment by the sound of laughter, he forgot himself so far as to let one hand drop from his face. In one peek he realized that all but he had their houses and their names on the board. On his little face, swollen and reddened by tears, I could see, for all his distress, his desire to be represented there as well.

I went toward him, a stick of chalk in my hand, ready to make up.

"Come on, Vincento, draw me the house where you live with your mother and daddy."

His disturbing eyes, burning under their long lashes, looked me in the face. I didn't know what to think about their expression, which was neither hostile nor trusting. I took another step toward him. Suddenly he was standing, and balanced on one foot he let go with the other as if it had been propelled by a steel spring. He caught me right on the shin with the tip of his cleated ankle-boot. This time I couldn't help making a face. Vincento seemed delighted. His back to the wall, crouching, he faced up to me, making it clear that between myself and him it could only be eye for eye and tooth for tooth.

"Very well," I said, "we don't need you," and I went off to busy myself with the other children, who, whether from kindness or a desire to make a good impression, showed signs of added affection.

In this way, and very quickly in spite of everything, the forenoon passed. After I had lined the children up in two's along the wall and opened the door for them, they began

15

going out in good order, without rushing, some even stopping to take my hand as they passed or to announce that they would be back in the afternoon; no one took flight, in any case. Except Vincento, who with a single bound dashed past the class and slipped outside with the speed of a weasel set free.

After lunch I came back to the school sick at heart. I'll have to start all over, I thought. Father and son will both be back in tears. I'll have to tear them apart again, chase one of them out and fight the other. My life as a teacher appeared to me in a devastating light. But I hurried back, hoping to arm myself for the coming struggle.

I arrived at one corner of the school. There, a few feet from the ground, was a window with a deep recess. I could make out a tiny form cowering in the shadow. God in heaven, could that be my little desperado come to take me in ambush?

The little shape poked its head out of cover. It was indeed Vincento. His shining eyes enveloped me in a look of passionate intensity. What was he planning? I had no more time to ask. He had sprung. He was at my feet like Friday at his master's. Then – and I still don't know how he did it – he climbed me as a cat climbs a tree, with knees that clamped first my hips and then my waist. His arms finally around my neck, he hugged until I thought I would choke. And he began to cover my face with great wet kisses that smelled of garlic and ravioli and liquorice. My face was all smeared with them. In vain, out of breath, I begged him: "Come, that's enough, Vincento. . . ." He hugged me with a strength that was incredible in such a small creature. And in my ear he poured a flood of words in Italian that seemed to me words of tenderness.

To make him let go I had to calm him slowly, little by little, with friendly pats on the back, hugging him in my turn and speaking to him affectionately in a language he knew

16

as little as I knew his; I had to cure the heart-rending fear he now seemed to have that he might lose me.

At last he let me put him down. He was trembling from this anxious but great happiness that had descended on him and found him still too small to bear its intensity. He took my hand and pulled me toward my classroom much faster than I had ever gone of my own volition.

He dragged me to my desk, took one for himself that was quite near, and sat down, his chin in his hands. And for lack of ability to tell me what he felt, he gave himself up totally to consuming me with his eyes.

And yet . . . afterwards . . . once that day of violence had passed . . . I don't remember much more about my little Vincento. The rest has melted, no doubt, into a general sweetness.

*C*hristmas was coming. My little pupils were getting more excited by the day. They would barely have copied the lesson from the board into their scribblers but they would be leaning over to one another in waves, whispering what they hoped to get from Santa Claus; or what they were going to give the teacher. I had done all I could to discourage these bursts of generosity toward me, as they were nearly always at the expense of parents. I found out that it could be harder to change the mind of a loving child than that of a grown man armed with all his strength.

While some of the children showed off, others with very poor parents were saddened that they would have nothing to give me. It was no use telling them that when they were nice to me, and when they worked hard, this was better than any present. They were inconsolable. And that year I'd had more trouble consoling one than all the others: little Clair.

That child was the best pupil you could have. He would go at the smallest task as if his life depended on it, or rather as if earning my approval was life itself to him.

19

While the children were busy copying the lesson from the blackboard I walked up and down the aisles, stopping to check each one's work; and often it was so badly done that I despaired of ever being good at my task. Everything changed when I examined Clair's book; for every day I marvelled at his fine, careful writing, or simply at his numbers lined up like a musical staff, in compact groups with even spaces between. He would have managed to make something attractive out of a page of straight lines. Every time I said to him – I couldn't help it, for it was as if when I praised him I was really reassuring myself about my calling – "My, you do good work, Clair!" the boy, still red-faced and tense from his efforts, would relax and thank me with such a gentle smile that I was almost ashamed to think of the heroic effort expended each day by this little fellow to get a good word from me. And I had to take care to give him something less than his due so as to avoid arousing envy and perhaps ill-will in the others.

In fact, I couldn't find a fault in him. He was open, able and intelligent; and what's more he was quiet, a rare quality in a gifted child. When he had finished his work, long before the others, instead of making noise or disturbing the class, he would stay quite still in his place and follow me around with his eyes, totally happy, as if that was already his reward. And I too came to glance often his way, and that, I suppose, was my reward.

From the beginning of the year he had worn the same suit of shiny, threadbare navy serge; but it was kept very clean and evidently scrubbed with vinegar water to reduce the shine, though the treatment hardly helped. Then one day the suit looked as good as new. I remarked on this to Clair, who explained that his mother had noticed the inside was barely worn, and had spent the weekend turning it inside out.

The sombre effect of the dark suit was relieved by a turned-down white collar which set off the oval of his face amid his fine, blond hair. Some of his companions had laughed at him because of this get-up, calling him a sissy or a mamma's boy, and the gently-brought-up child had not been able to understand why they laughed. One day, shortly after, I found a picture of a boys' choir in dark suits and white collars, and I imagined that Clair's mother had perhaps seen the same picture and copied the dress for her son. I cut it out and pinned it up at the front of the class. From then on Clair seemed to be not quite the only one of his species among us, though he was as timid as ever.

It happened one day – I wish I could forget it – that I was very tired and lost patience, to the point of giving a push to one of the boys for no good reason. The victim was not the most affected, however. Out of habit I glanced at Clair, questioning, and I saw the consternation on his face. Gradually, in this way, the boy became a kind of highly reliable guide to me. If his eyes sparkled with interest I could be sure that my lesson had been well-conducted. If they filled with tears it was because I had found the right tone to touch his heart. If he laughed out loud with a happy cascade of bells I knew that my attempts at the comic had also succeeded.

But now, at the approach of Christmas, nothing could cheer him up. If he still sang with the others, because he had to, it was without vibrancy, and his sad little voice could hardly be heard in the choir. He no longer smiled when it came to the "Ding, dong, ding!" He still wrote just as carefully in his notebook, which his mother had bound with brown paper to keep it clean; but if I leaned over as usual to say, "That's very well done, Clair . . ." his suffering seemed to grow, so that I almost stopped praising him altogether. And finally even avoided his loving gaze.

By the week before Christmas the children could no longer contain themselves. They wanted to give me a surprise, but still more to tell me what my presents would be. Petit-Louis was underfoot half the time, keeping me up-to-date on his progress in persuading his father to shell out a box of chocolates for me. "A two-pound one, that's the hard part," he declared.

Petit-Louis was the son of a frail little Polish Jew who had come to our city to open one of those wretched stores whose stock, from lack of space or negligence, was in a permanent mess: on the floor, in corners or in a jumbled heap behind the sooty windows, candies lying among the soap and cornflakes. I wasn't anxious to get chocolates that had come from that store, but how to stop Petit-Louis?

"My father," he said, "he's almost ready to give in for a one-pound box. But that's not what I want. What I want for that teacher, and I told him so, I want two pounds."

"But one's enough, you know. And shush! Not so loud, Louis. Not all the children have a father who can give chocolates away."

But Louis loved me in his own way. He started up again, his nose running, his voice whining as if it had been forever trained in haggling:

"I told my father, if you don't give me a two-pound box you can find somebody else to deliver after four. I need two pounds. One pound," he insisted, "isn't good enough."

Then Johnny, whose father worked on the sewers in summer and was unemployed in winter, came along with the loud "secret" that his mother was knitting me slippers with ends of wool of all colours which she had managed to save. But he had to keep a good eye on her, for she was likely as not to drop the knitting and go have fun somewhere.

"My mother's lazy," he informed me. "Look at yesterday, she left everything and went playing cards in broad daylight."

"You don't say things like that about your mother, Johnny! Come on!"

"But it's true! My own father said so! She's a big

22

lazybones, my mother is! But I'm not going to let her alone till she's finished your slippers!''

There was no denying it. My pupils with their angelic faces turned into little monsters at Christmas, determined to bleed their parents in order to be generous to me. I lectured them and told them it wasn't nice to pester their poor parents, who had trouble enough buying what their family needed, and you mustn't, Louis . . . and you shouldn't, Johnny . . . But it was no use. Louis didn't let up on his father, but kept me up-to-date.

"He's almost ready for the two pounds, but it's not a sure thing yet. He's stingy with his chocolate. What a shame! For at wholesale price it doesn't cost him that much.''

Johnny, for his part, had to report that his mother had lost the slipper she'd started, but she'd better find it or he'd make it hot for her.

"She's just careless," he said.

"Johnny!''

"My dad said so.''

Even my charming little Nikolai started bothering his mother because of me. The family lived on the edge of the city dump, where they'd had no trouble in finding building materials (rusted corrugated iron, old bed-frames and planks that were still sound) for a rather pleasant cabin, especially in summer when it was surrounded by flowers and chickens. I knew where it was. In September, as soon as he had fallen in love with me, Nikolai had no rest until he'd dragged me there after class one afternoon, to see how nice it was at his place. His mother grew real flowers in summertime and in winter made them of fine cloth or paper and sold them very cheaply to the big stores who sold them dear. From this ill-heated cabin came jonquils so delicately made that you wanted to sniff them like real flowers.

Anastasia, Nikolai's mother, sometimes put a drop of perfume in the heart of the flower.

23

"At least three flowers, that's what I want for you," said Nikolai. "D'you think that's enough?"

"Too many, Nikolai. Just think how long it takes your mother to make a single flower. And she doesn't get that much for them!"

"All right, then, one," he said sadly. "At least one. But one isn't much."

"On the contrary. One is better. You can see it properly, you can't help seeing it."

"Oh? Do you think so?"

But the next day he came to tell me not to get my hopes up.

"You know, even one flower – I'm not sure you'll get one. My father doesn't want it. He watches out like a fox. As soon as she's made a few flowers he takes them and runs and sells them. We never see them again. Yesterday there were some beautiful red geraniums, and they're gone. If I can steal one for you," he asked, giving me a caress, "what kind would you like me to steal? Lilies of the valley? Sweet peas? Lilac? My little mother makes lilacs best of all. She get the most money for them. But they take longest to make."

"Oh, nothing at all, Nikolai! You break my heart, talking about stealing your mother's work."

"She mightn't ever notice," said Nikolai, in his tenderness for me. "Sometimes I swipe a cookie when they're still hot and she only laughs."

After these effusions and confidences – which at times quite put me off Christmas, a hard feast for loving hearts – I would look Clair's way. From where he sat he missed nothing of these noisy demonstrations but made not the slightest effort to take part in them, except with his eyes which at times were fixed on me, full of regret, only to look down again as if in shame.

He too, I thought, must be pressuring his mother. I had never seen her. But it happened that from one child or another I had some notion of what the mother was like.

24

Thus, I had liked Nikolai's as soon as he began to tell me about her. And no doubt I was inclined toward Clair's mother. But I began to think it strange that she had never shown up.

The next days were terribly cold. Several children missed school. But not Clair. When I arrived a little late that day, I found him already at his desk, practising aloud the day's reading lesson.

He broke off and stood up to greet me in the way I had asked the children to greet visitors: no doubt because he thought, having arrived before me, that he was bound to observe the rule for my benefit as well. We said a good day to each other, and he sat down again and went on with his reading:

Jack and Jill
Went up the hill . . .

in such a sad voice that I can still hear it, forever linked to a generous child's first great sorrow. I would have done anything to free him from it, but that would have meant depriving him of the affection he felt for me, and that was the last thing I wanted.

That morning, with almost half the children absent, I could have taken as much time as I liked to pay special attention to him, but I didn't dare. I may even have given him a little less than usual.

We were going to have a few minutes recess when I saw in the glass door-panel a gentle, timid face. I went and opened the door. I found before me a woman in a worn coat that gaped to reveal a dark dress adorned with a collar so clean that suddenly one saw no more than its exquisite whiteness. Her eyes were of a blue that I recognized, perhaps a little paler, as if faded by the effects of life. I held out my hands to her.

"You must surely be Clair's mother!"

In thanks for having known her she gave me the same tender smile as her little boy when he was touched, then remembered to excuse herself for having bothered me during class. She had washed Clair's mittens the night before, she explained, and they hadn't had time to dry during the night. So she had tried to dissuade Clair from coming to school this morning because of the extreme cold, but nothing doing, he left with bare hands. And then the lady she was doing housework for today saw that she was upset because of the mittens, and gave her a few minutes off to bring them to Clair.

She gave them to me, remarking that they were still a shade damp, but if I put them on the radiator they'd have plenty of time to dry before school was out. She said she'd be most grateful if I would see to that, for then she could go away reassured; it was no use telling Clair to keep his hands in his pockets, he might forget, or maybe decide to bring home his notebook to show her, and he could freeze his hands and never notice. . . . At that age you had no idea . . .

I told her I would see to the mittens, and she needn't worry about them anymore.

Then, on the point of leaving, she hesitated, and suddenly took upon herself to ask if I was satisfied with her little boy, was he obedient and polite, because – she said – she had very little time to give him, as she had to earn a living for the two of them doing housework here and there, and often worried that Clair might resent the fact and not be as much of a gentleman as she would have wished.

"A gentleman! But he couldn't be more so!"

"Oh! Truly now?"

She seemed relieved of a part of her fatigue and worry, though in her modesty far from certain that Clair was as perfect as I said. Yet she wanted to believe it, and murmured:

"Well, if you say so! You're the one who said so!"

But it was obvious that she still had a weight on her heart, and suddenly, there on the doorstep, seeking the encouragement of my eyes, she confided hastily:

"Sometimes I'm afraid of not doing right by him. I'm alone to bring him up. His father left us."

I took her hands. I held out my arms to this woman who was able to draw so much sweetness from her troubles.

When I returned to my desk I realized that Clair had seen me embrace his mother and that he had been touched as one is on seeing that two dear ones are fond of each other. He was radiant, and for once forgetful of his work, thinking about what had happened, the tip of his tongue emerging to taste – you could imagine – a touch of honey on his lip. To see him happy made me happy too. Alas, but not for long! In the end his joy only fed his pain, when he rediscovered it on a sidetrack of his thoughts. Then he looked sadder than ever. When I paid him a little compliment on something or other, I saw that he was ready to weep. A simple friendly glance from me set his chin trembling.

The weather grew less severe. It snowed. Just the way it should for Christmas: a soft, abundant snow that covered everything afresh and rejoiced the eyes of my small pupils. They liked nothing better than coming to school under these floating flakes that they tried to catch on the fly with half-opened lips, or in their palms, turned to the sky. They brought with them the good smell of furry little animals coming in from the cold. Sometimes, intact on their eyelashes or on a sleeve, I would find an immense snowflake shaped like a star. I would take it off with care to show this marvel to the child who had brought it.

My pupils, with their joy, brought back my own childhood. To complete the circle, I tried to magnify their joy so that it would go with them all through their lives.

We came to the day before Christmas Eve. It was the last day of the term. I passed out my presents, more or less the same for everyone: a handful of candies, three or four

27

walnuts, a niggertoe, an apple or an orange, and a little tin whistle or some such trinket.

A few days before Christmas, we teachers of the beginner classes enjoyed getting together after four in one of our classrooms to wrap our gifts for the children. In this way we all took advantage of the notions of the most ingenious, from year to year taking increasing pains to give a pretty wrapping to our modest presents which in those hard times were, for more than one child, the only gift he would receive.

I had invented a game to make the distribution of the presents more suspenseful for my pupils. This time, once again, I told them:

"I've just met a mysterious visitor. He'll be here any moment. On his back he has a big bag full of presents for you. But this visitor doesn't like to be seen. Secrecy is his happiness and mystery his friend. Now you must lay your head on your arms, on the desk, hiding your face and pretending to sleep. And mind: no cheating, no opening an eye! The visitor would see it and might leave you nothing!"

The children got in the spirit of the game. They shut their eyes tight. (One year, when the presents were all given out, I had had to waken one of my little ones who had actually gone to sleep, his head on his desk.) I took the presents from my big drawer and tiptoed, my arms full, up and down the aisles, leaving a present by each little "sleeping" head.

Then I went to the door, opened it, and said softly, as if to someone leaving: "Thank you for coming. The children will be glad. I want to thank you for them. Have a good trip, my friend! See you next year!"

I shut the door and announced aloud to the children: "There! He's gone. Now look and see what the unknown visitor brought you!"

In great haste the children tore open the paper cones I

28

had spent hours making and tying with ribbon. There were Oh's and Ah's everywhere, for the children were as gifted as we teachers were in heightening tone and gesture at this time of year.

I watched Clair slowly undoing his package. He remained silent as he gazed at what it contained, then finally raised his eyes to me with a strange look in which his grateful nature underlined still more the sadness of a little boy with empty hands.

For it goes without saying that his companions, starting that morning, had almost all presented me with a gift, or what could pass for one, with a hundred kinds of coyness – Petit-Louis, with no wrapping paper, nothing, a naked box of chocolates, one-pound, grumbling: "My father will pay for this. I told him two pounds I want for that teacher, that's what I want, I told him. . . ." And Johnny, with a pair of slippers that looked as if they were both made for the same foot, and so small that I wondered if they weren't "mine for me" rather than "yours for you." Ossip brought a picture of the Virgin of Perpetual Help, which he pulled all wrinkled from his pocket, trying to smooth it out with his hand, and explaining that this was a powerful Lady who would give you almost anything you asked for – and it didn't matter if she was old, old, old, did it? As long as she gave people what they wanted? And I assured him that indeed it didn't matter if she was old and even irreparably wrinkled if she had the power to give a hand to people on this earth; and finally Tascona who, before he got my apple, offered me his, but not without taking a tiny bite just out of one corner, so to speak.

The highlight of the day, however, had been the arrival of a kind of giant with yellow moustaches, in a rabbit-skin hat and high boots, carrying under his arm a clumsy package from which he extracted three roses with long stems and smooth, small leaves. He put them in my hands and left without turning his back to me, repeating:

29

"Anastasia sends . . . Anastasia sends . . . And may the newborn Christ take you in his holy safekeeping."

I had found a slim vase to put them in, and they stood among three sprigs of fine greenery on my desk in a ray of sunlight, so like their live sisters that two of my fellow-teachers coming in cried: "Roses! You're the lucky one!"

And lucky I was to have caught the look on Nikolai's face when his father arrived: such a thrill that I thought the child would choke with happiness.

From that moment on he was in paradise, and had done nothing but contemplate the three roses. He emerged from his dream just long enough to come and move the vase on my desk so that the roses might stay in the sun.

Then came the time for us to separate for the holidays. The children, dressed for the outdoors, were nicely lined up along the wall, ready to leave, each with his present under his arm. Through the windows you could see the snow, which hadn't stopped for two days, flying past in flurries. The atmosphere was in a stormy mood. As always, before letting the little ones out in bad weather, I went down the line to make sure that coats were buttoned to the top and scarves in place. Often there was a last-minute search for stray mittens. I went from one to the next, pulling the scarf up higher, unbuttoning a coat that was done up crookedly and buttoning it up the right way, noticing here and there, "Hey! You're missing a button, better get your mother to sew it on again right away . . ." I took advantage of this process to wish a Merry Christmas to each child and thank him for his gift. "Thanks, Petit-Louis, I'm going to have a real feast on your chocolates. Two pounds would have been far too much, really. Thanks to you and your daddy. Thank you too, Ossip, for the Virgin that gives everything. She'll be a real help to me. Thank you, Tony, for your lovely round apple . . . and Nikolai for the roses. I think

I'll not let them stay all alone in the school during the holidays. I'm taking them home." With joy, Nikolai took my hand and kissed it, then asked:

"Are you pleased? Really pleased?"

"I couldn't be more so, Nikolai."

I came to Clair. His lashes were holding back the tears. I re-tied his blue wool scarf. I made sure his mittens were there, hanging from a knitted string that went behind his neck and descended the inside of each sleeve. I made him put them on at once and couldn't help noticing that they were getting worn thin and hadn't much warmth left in them. He was trembling as I did him up, and I took him by the shoulders.

"Would you like," I said, "to give me the nicest present in the world?"

Clair, not understanding what I could be expecting of him now, but quick as ever to respond to my slightest wish, nodded his head.

"Fine! What I'd like is to see this little boy give me a happy smile."

The child looked at me from the depths of his sorrow, and as his tears fell, on his lips flowered a tender and adorable smile.

What a storm Christmas gave us that year! It filled the air with moaning, that ancient distress of the depth of winter, and perhaps as well with bitter mockery: "What! You're still hoping? Still and always! And for how long now! How long?"

The snow no longer fell in those filigree flakes that, in their ephemeral beauty, I had been able to pluck alive from the children's eyelashes, but it had become a terrified fugitive to which the wind gave no rest for an instant.

In this tempest, nothing familiar was left to our eyes but the telephone poles emerging for a second at a time, tall,

31

gaunt walkers standing up to the gusts, not losing an inch of ground.

My mother, my sister and I were the only ones at home. Death had taken many of our family, and life had scattered the rest to the four winds.

Several times my mother had gone to the window, looked out and complained:

"In weather like this not a soul's going to come by!"

"Who on earth could come?"

She cast a melancholy glance my way and gave no explanation. And I wondered what an old mother, who has lost almost all that life had given her so abundantly, can still expect at Christmas time?

For that matter, what do we expect, all of us, perpetually disappointed as we are, and always ready to start again?

Without really noticing what I was doing, I too went to look out and grumble:

"You wouldn't send a cat out on a day like this."

All at once, through the shrill piping of the wind, we thought we heard the muffled sound of our doorbell.

"It must be a trick of the wind," said mother. "Or a loose wire. Go and see anyway."

I opened the door. On the step there was indeed someone waiting. A little creature white with snow, wrapped in so much wool to cover him against the evil weather that he had lost his human form. I lowered the scarf from across his face. Those were surely Clair's blue eyes. Dancing with joy. Under his arm he pressed a small package.

"Come in, quickly. You must be cold through and through. Going out in that weather, how could your mother let you? Take your things off."

But first he held out the little package, saying:

"Merry Christmas . . . and this is from my mother and me."

I helped him get out of I don't know how many jackets and sweaters. At the end there emerged the familiar little manikin in his blue suit as good as new, with the white collar freshly washed and starched. He sat down in the middle of our big sofa. I had never seen his eyes shine like this. I offered him a piece of cake. No? A glass of milk then? He was bursting with impatience for me to open the package which for the moment lay in my lap.

My mother appeared then, and stopped in the doorway, delighted by the sight of this child among us. On that day, at that hour, did he not bring back a little of the childhood of so many of her own children now grown old, ill or vanished into death?

Clair stood up and wished her:

"Merry Christmas, Mrs. Mother Teacher!"

I undid the parcel, with its used wrapping paper (the new folds didn't quite match the old ones). From its thin box I drew out a fine linen handkerchief with a tiny green sticker attesting to its Irish origin. Though spotlessly clean it was not quite new. It had that gentle tint of pale ivory, a little sad, taken on by white linen after a time, even when stored with the greatest care. Where, I wondered, for all those years, had it been awaiting its strange destination? I imagined that one of the ladies where Clair's mother worked had perhaps on Christmas eve remembered this handkerchief forgotten for so long in a drawer somewhere, and said: "There, now! That's something I could give the poor woman!"

My mother cried:

"And you were just wishing for an Irish linen hankie!"

I held it up to my face, and said to Clair:

"It's as soft as a cloud!"

The child's happiness, though silent, made me think of a vibrant trumpet blast. Now he was willing to eat. My mother brought him a piece of cake so big that I re-

33

proached her: "Do you want to make him sick?" To which she replied: "At his age, and then with the walk back in that wild wind. . . ."

Clair, sitting in the middle of the sofa, ate properly with his fork. His tongue was loosened. He told us about the splendid Christmas they were having, his mother and he, as they'd both had gifts from a very kind lady for whom his mother had been cleaning for some time. Right now their dinner was in the oven, cooking slowly. Yet he didn't seem in a hurry to leave us.

We listened to his little voice, overexcited by too much joy and emotion, as if it would never stop. I had to remind him that his mother was certainly going to be worried to death until she saw him back again. He admitted then that she had told him not to be too long.

I helped him bundle up. I noticed that today he had two pairs of mittens, one over the other, the old ones which I knew, and brand-new ones with a complicated design in brilliant colours. He spread the new mittens out for me to admire. They were the ones he wore on top.

"They're from my mother. She finished them last night. It takes long to knit them because of so many colours, and you have to use them all at once and not mix them up."

"Yes, and I never saw such pretty ones. But the present you brought me is even better. You were right not to give it to me in front of the other children. They might have been jealous."

Clair gave me a penetrating look to be sure I wasn't just saying that to please him, and in his joy at believing me he suddenly seemed gifted with wings.

I opened the door.

"Take good care you don't get lost. Follow the telephone poles."

Under the scarf that half covered his face I heard him laughing and making gentle fun of me:

34

"My mother said that too. Everybody says to follow the poles."

Away he went in the tempest, like a little goat leaping through the maddened snow. Above his head his hand traced signs of friendship in the air, and I thought I heard him sing out: Good-bye! Good-bye!

Good-bye indeed, little Clair! Good-bye until next Christmas! Good-bye until every Christmas in the world!

*Q*uite often I asked my small pupils to sing together. One day, in the midst of their rather colourless voices, I could make out one that was clear, vibrant and astonishingly accurate. I had the group stop and let Nil go on alone. What a ravishing voice, and how precious to me, who had never had much of an ear for music!

From then on I would ask: "Nil, will you give the note?"

He would do so without coaxing and without pride - a child born to sing as others are born to pout.

The rest, my flight of sparrows, took off in his wake, soon following rather well; for besides his rare talent, Nil seemed able to pass it on to the others. We listened to him and believed we too could sing.

My music hour was the envy of the teachers in neighbouring classrooms.

"What's going on? We're getting a concert from your room every day now!"

They couldn't believe it, for I had never before shone as a singing teacher.

Our old inspector was stupefied when he came around.

"What's this? Your children are singing a thousand times better than other years!"

Then he stopped staring suspiciously at me, and asked to have them sing once more; and first thing I knew he was off in a happy reverie in which he seemed not even to remember that he was a school inspector.

Shortly after this visit I had another from our principal, who said in a faintly sarcastic way:

"I understand your children are such fine singers this year. I'm very curious to hear these little angels. Would you ask them to perform for me?"

Our principal was a little man made somewhat taller by his crest of blond hair, combed up in the middle like the picture of Monsieur Thiers in the dictionary. His dress, which was that of our teaching brothers at the time, was also very impressive: a black frock-coat and a white, starched dickey.

I had the pupils come close in a compact group, with Nil, one of the smallest, almost hidden in the middle. I made a little sign to him. He gave the starting tone just loudly enough to be heard by those around him. A wire vibrating harmoniously somewhere near! And the choir took off with such zest and in such perfect unison that I thought: Even the principal must be dazzled by this!

At any rate the mocking smile vanished quickly from his face. In its place appeared, to my amazement, the same expression of happy reverie, as if he had forgotten that he was a manager always busy running his school.

Hands behind his back, he wagged his head gently in rhythm with the tune and even when the song was ended kept on listening to it in his mind a moment longer.

But he had spotted the captivating voice. He brought Nil out of the group, looked long and attentively at him, and patted him on the cheek.

As I accompanied him to the door, he said:

38

"Well, with your thirty-eight sparrows you've caught a meadowlark this year. Do you know the lark? Let him sing and there's not a heart but is lightened!"

I suppose I was too young myself to know what a lightened heart was. But I soon had some idea of it.

That day had started very badly, under a driving autumn rain. The children arrived at school wet, sniffling and ill-humoured, with enormous muddy feet that soon turned my schoolroom, which I loved to see sparkling clean, into a kind of stable. As soon as I went to pick up a still-intact clod of black earth, two or three children would make a point of crushing others with their toes, scattering them in the aisles, watching me slyly all the while. I hardly recognized my pupils in these little rebels who would have risen against me at the drop of a hat, and perhaps they didn't recognize in me their beloved school mistress of yesterday. What had happened to turn us into something resembling enemies?

Some of our most experienced colleagues blamed the moments before the storm, the children's delicate nerves being strained by the atmospheric tension; and some said it was the long school days following weekends or holidays. After that taste of freedom the return to school was like going back to jail; and they grew quite disobedient, and all the more excitable, fidgety and impossible because they felt in their bones, poor things, that their revolt against the adult world had not the slightest chance of ultimate success.

It was my turn to have one of those dreadful days when the teacher seems to be there to do nothing but scold, and the children to comply, and all the sadness in the world settles into this place which can be so happy at other times.

As the bad weather kept up, instead of working off this excess nervousness in the open air we had to go to the gym in the basement, where shoes were loud on the hard floor.

The children fought about nothing. I had to treat split lips and bloody noses.

Afterwards, fresh from a visit to the toilets, the children left their desks one after the other to ask permission to go down again. Impossible to continue with my lesson in that traffic! One would leave, another would just be coming back, the door would open, a draught would blow scribblers to the floor and they'd be picked up covered with dirt, and the door would slam: another child was going out. Suddenly I could take no more. "No! That will do! There's a limit after all."

Now it happened that without thinking, but as if I had done it on purpose, my "no" fell on little Charlie, a gentle child, quite guileless, whom his mother purged two or three times a year with a mixture of sulphur and molasses. Relegated to his desk, Charlie couldn't hold in very long. The odour gave him away to his neighbours, little monsters who pretended to be shocked, and shouted from where they sat, as if it wasn't obvious enough: "Charlie did it in his pants." In haste I had to write a note to his mother whom I knew to be vindictive, while Charlie stood at my desk, his legs apart, whimpering with shame.

I hadn't long to wait for the consequences. Charlie had been gone a half-hour when the principal showed his head in the high glass of the door and gestured that he wanted to speak to me. It was a serious business when he called us out to the corridor. Charlie's mother, he told me, had phoned. She was so furious that he had trouble persuading her not to sue me. Laugh if you please, there was such a thing as parents suing a teacher for less than that, and I was accused of having obliged Charlie's mother to re-wash his underwear, which she had done only yesterday.

I tried to present the facts from my point of view, but the principal remarked with some severity that it was better to let the whole class go to the toilet for nothing than to prevent one child in real need.

40

Perhaps because I was ashamed of myself, I tried to make the children ashamed at having shown their worst possible side all day. They weren't in the least contrite; quite the contrary – they seemed very pleased with themselves indeed, for the most part.

I went and sat down, completely discouraged. And the future descended on me, making all my years to come resemble this one day. I could see myself in twenty, thirty years, still in the same place, worn down by my task, the very image of the "oldest" of my present colleagues whom I found so pitiful; and thinking of them, my pity turned on myself. It goes without saying that the children took advantage of my dejection to chase each other up and down the aisles and add to the tumult. My glance fell on little Nil. While almost all the children were running amok, he was at his desk, trying to concentrate on his drawing. Apart from singing, what interested him most was to draw a cabin, always the same cabin, surrounded by curious animals, with chickens as tall as his cows.

I called to him, I think as if for help:

"Nil, come here a second."

He came running. He was a funny little manikin and always oddly dressed. On this day a pair of men's braces, barely shortened, held up pants that were too big, their crotch hanging to his knees. His boots must have been just as oversized, for I heard them clatter as he ran up. With his mop of tow-coloured hair and his square head, flat on the top, he looked like a good little kulak determined to get an education. In fact, when he wasn't singing he was the last one in the class that you'd take for a meadowlark.

He leaned toward me affectionately.

"What do you want?"

"To talk to you. Tell me, who taught you to sing so well?"

"My mother."

I had glimpsed her once when the report cards were

given out: a gentle, embarrassed smile, high cheekbones like Nil's, fine, penetrating eyes under her snow-white kerchief, a timid shadow who left as she had come, in silence. Did she know more than a few words apart from her own Ukrainian tongue?

"So she teaches you in Ukrainian?"

"Why, sure!"

"Do you know many Ukrainian songs?"

"Hundreds!"

"So many?"

"Well, at least ten . . . or twelve."

"Would you sing us one?"

"Which one?"

"Any one you like."

He took up a firm stand as if to resist the wind, his feet wide apart, his head thrown back, his eyes already shining, in a transformation more radical than I had ever seen – the first time he had sung at school in his mother's language: a little rustic turned into one possessed by music. His body swayed to a catchy rhythm, his shoulders went up, his eyes flamed, and a smile from time to time parted his slightly fleshy lips. With raised hand he seemed to point with a graceful gesture at some pretty scene in the distance, and you couldn't help following the gesture to see what it was he found so pleasing. I couldn't tell which was better: listening to him with my eyes closed, to enjoy that splendid voice without distraction; or watching him sing, so lively, so playful, as if he were ready to rise from the earth.

When this delightful song was ended we were in another world. The children had gradually gone back to their seats. I was no longer in despair about my future. Nil's singing had turned my heart inside out like a glove. Now I was confident about life.

I asked Nil: "Have you any idea what the song's about?"

"Sure I have!"

"Could you explain it to us?"

He launched into the story:

"There's a tree. It's a cherry tree in bloom. In the country my mother comes from there's lots of them. This cherry tree, it's in the middle of a field. Some young girls are dancing around it. They're waiting for the boys that are in love with them."

"What a lovely story!"

"Yes, but it's going to be sad," said Nil, "for one of the boys was killed in the war."

"Oh, that's too bad!"

"No, because that gives a chance to another fellow who was secretly in love with her, and he's the good guy."

"Oh! Fine! But where did your mother learn these songs?"

"In that country, before they left, when she was a little girl. Now she says that's all we have left from the Ukraine."

"And she's hurrying to get all that into your little head so it's your turn to keep it?"

He looked at me gravely to be very sure of what I had said, then he smiled affectionately.

"I won't lose a one," he said. And then, "Would you like me to sing another one?"

My mother had broken a hip about three months before. She had been immobilized in a plaster corset for a long time. The doctor had finally removed it and asserted that she would be able to walk if she persevered. She made a great effort every day, but couldn't manage to move her bad leg. I had seen her losing hope during the last week or two. I would catch her sitting in her armchair by the window looking at the outdoors with an expression of heartrending regret. I would scold her so that she wouldn't think I was worried about her. Lively, active and independent as she was, what would her life be if she spent the rest

43

of it a cripple? The horror I had felt one day at the thought of being chained for a lifetime to my teacher's desk gave me a glimpse of her feelings at the prospect of never leaving her prisoner's lookout at the window.

One day I had the notion of bringing Nil home to entertain her, for she found the days "deathly long."

"Would you like to come home, Nil, and sing for *my* mother? She's lost all her songs!"

He had a way of saying yes without a word, placing his little hand in mine as if to tell me: You know very well I'd go to the world's end with you. And it went straight to my heart.

On the way I explained to him that my mother was much older than his, and that it was hard at her age to get back her lost confidence. I still don't know what possessed me to get into explanations of that kind with a child of six and a half. But he listened, deadly serious, trying with all his might to fathom what I expected of him.

When my mother, who had just had a nap, opened her eyes and saw beside her this manikin in his wide braces, she must have thought he was one of the poor kids I had so often brought home so that she could make them a coat or alter one to their size. She said a little bitterly, but more in sadness, I think, at no longer being able to help:

"What's this? You know I can't sew anymore, except little things I can do by hand."

"No, no, it's not that. It's a surprise. Listen."

I made a sign to Nil. He planted himself in front of my mother as if to resist a strong wind, and launched into the happy song of the cherry tree. His body swayed, his eyes sparkled, a smile came to his lips, his little hand rose up to point, far beyond this sickroom, to what? A highway? A plain? Some open landscape, anyway, that he made you want to see.

When he had finished he looked at my mother, who said not a word, hiding her gaze from him. He suggested:

"D'you want to hear another one of my songs?"

My mother, as if from a distance, nodded her head, without showing her face, which stayed hidden behind her hand.

Nil sang another song, and this time my mother held her head high, watching the smiling child; and with his help she too was away, taking flight far above life, on the wings of a dream.

That evening she asked me to bring her a strong kitchen chair with a high back and help her stand up behind it, using it as a support.

I suggested that the chair could slip and pull her forward, so she had me lay a heavy dictionary on it.

With this strange "walker" of her own invention my mother resumed her exercises. Weeks passed and I could see no change. I was growing completely discouraged. My mother too, no doubt, for she seemed to have given up. What I didn't know was that, having realized she was on the point of succeeding, she had decided to go on with her exercises in secret so as to give me a surprise. A surprise it was! I was in the blackest despondency that evening when I heard her shout from her room:

"I'm walking! I can walk!"

I ran to her. My mother, pushing the chair in front of her, was progressing with tiny mechanical steps, like those of a wind-up doll, and she kept up her cry of triumph:

"I can walk! I can walk!"

Of course I don't claim that Nil performed a miracle. But perhaps he gave a little puff at just the right time to the flickering faith of my mother.

However that may be, this experiment gave me the urge to try another.

The previous year I had gone along with one of my colleagues and a group of her pupils who were putting on a little play for the old people in a home in our town.

45

Of all the prisons that human beings forge for themselves or are forced to suffer, not one, even today, seems as intolerable as the one in which we are confined by age. I had sworn never again to set foot in that home; it had upset me so. Maybe during the year I had made some progress in compassion, for here I was thinking of taking Nil there. He seemed the only one likely to be able to comfort the old people I had seen immured in the institution.

I spoke to the principal who thought for a long time and then said the idea had its good points . . . very good points, but first I'd have to get permission from the mother.

I set about writing a letter to Nil's mother, in which I said something to the effect that the songs she had brought from the Ukraine and passed on to her son seemed to be beneficial to the people here, as perhaps they had been to her own people . . . helping them to live . . . And would she please lend me Nil for an evening that might go on rather late?

I read it to Nil, asking him to get it firmly into his head because he would have to read it at home and give an exact translation to his mother. He listened attentively and as soon as I had finished asked if I'd like him to repeat it word for word, just to be sure that he had memorized it. I said that wouldn't be necessary, that I had faith in his memory.

Next day Nil brought me the reply on a piece of paper cut out from a brown paper bag. It was in telegraphic style:

"We lend Nil to the old people."

It was signed in letters that looked like embroidery:

Paraskovia Galaïda.

"What a beautiful name your mother has!" I said to Nil, trying to read it properly.

And on hearing my odd pronunciation, he burst out laughing in my face.

The old people's home had its own little auditorium, with a

46

platform two steps high lit by a row of weak footlights which isolated it from the audience.

Caught in a beam of golden light, Nil was charming to see with his straw-coloured hair and the Ukrainian blouse with its embroidered collar, which his mother had made him wear. For my own part I missed a little seeing my manikin with the wide braces. On his face with its high cheekbones you could already see the joy he felt at the idea of singing. From my hiding place, where if need be I could prompt him as to what to do, I could see the audience as well as the stage, and it was among them, you might have thought, that the real drama was being played – that of life saying its last word.

In the first row was an old man afflicted with a convulsive palsy, like an apple tree that someone had shaken, still trembling long after its last fruit had fallen. Somewhere someone was breathing with a whistling sound like wind caught inside a hollow tree. Another old man tried to keep up with his lungs in a race with death. Near the middle of the room was one, half paralyzed, whose living eyes in his inert face had an unbearable lucidity. There was a poor woman, swollen to an enormous mass of flesh. And no doubt there were those who were still unscathed, if that happy chance consisted here of simply being worn, wrinkled, shrunken and eroded by some process of unimaginable ferocity. When is old age at its most atrocious: when you are in it, like these people in the home? – or seen from afar, through the eyes of tender youth that could wish for death at the sight?

Then, in that day's end, the clear, radiant voice of Nil rose as if from the shining morning of life. He sang of the flowering cherry tree, of the girls in love dancing their round on the plain, of the expectations of youthful hearts. With a gesture that was charmingly at ease he would raise his hand and point to a distant road to be followed . . . or a far horizon which, from his shining eyes, you imagined

47

must be luminous. At one moment his lips parted in a smile that was so contagious it leapt over the footlights and appeared in all its fresh sweetness on the aged faces. He sang about Petrushka's adventure, and how he was caught by his own trickery. He sang a song that I had never heard, a gentle, melancholy song about the Dnieper River running on and on, bearing laughter and sighs, hopes and regrets, down toward the sea, until at the end everything melts into the eternal waves.

I didn't know the old people; they had changed so. In the dark evening of their lives this ray of morning had broken through to them. The palsied man succeeded in holding still a moment so as to hear more clearly. The eye of the paralytic no longer wandered, searching, calling for help, but turned and fixed upon Nil so as to see him as well as possible. The man who had been chasing his own breathing seemed to be holding his breath with his two hands clasped across his chest in a marvellous respite from his affliction. They all looked happy now, hanging on the next notes from Nil. And the tragic spectacle of the audience ended in a kind of parody, with old men excited as children, some on the verge of laughter, others of tears, because they were rediscovering so vividly in themselves the traces of what was lost.

Then I said to myself that this was, after all, too cruel, and I would never again bring Nil here to sing and reawaken hope.

How the renown of my little healer of the ills of life began to spread, I have no idea, but soon I was getting requests from all sides.

One day, through the high glass door-panel, the principal made a sign that he wanted to talk to me.

"This time," he said, "it's a psychiatric hospital that's asking for our little Ukrainian lark. This is a serious question, and we must think it over."

48

Yes, it was serious, but once again, and as if it were beyond my own will, my decision had been made. If Paraskovia Galaïda gave her permission I would go with Nil to see the "madmen," as people called them then.

She agreed, with no trouble. I wonder now if she even worried about where we went. She seemed to have as much confidence in me as Nil did.

In the mental hospital also there was a little auditorium with a low platform, but without any bank of footlights or spots to separate this side from that. Everything was bathed in the same dull, uniform light. If the world of the aged in the home had made me think of tragedy's last act, here I had the impression of an epilogue mimed by shadows that had already passed on to a kind of death.

The patients were seated in docile ranks, most of them apathetic, their eyes bleak, twiddling their thumbs or biting at their lips.

Nil made his entrance on the narrow platform of the stage. There was a rustle of surprise in the audience. A few patients even grew excited at this marvellous apparition – a child, here! One of them, over-agitated, pointed his finger at him in a kind of joyous bewilderment, as if asking others to confirm what his eyes were seeing.

Nil took up his position, his feet apart, a lock of hair hanging over his forehead, his hands on his hips, for he was going to start with "Kalinka" which he had just learned from his mother. He caught its devilish rhythm with fiery charm.

From the very first notes there was a silence such as you would feel when the forest hushes to hear a birdsong somewhere on a distant branch.

Nil was swaying, filled with an irresistible liveliness, sometimes tracing a gentle curve with his hand, sometimes passionately clapping both hands together. The patients followed his movements in ecstasy. And always this silence, as if in adoration.

"Kalinka" ended. Nil explained in a few words, as I had taught him, the meaning of the next song. He did this with complete ease, no more nervous than if he had been in class among his companions. Then he launched into his music again as if he would never grow tired of singing.

Now the patients were breathing together audibly, like a single, unhappy monster moving in the shadows, dreaming of its own release.

Nil went from one song to another, one sad, the next one gay. He no more saw the madmen than he had seen the aged, the sick, the sorrowful, with their torments of body and soul. He sang of the sweet, lost land of his mother which she had given him to keep, its prairies, its trees, a lone horseman crossing the distant plain. He ended with that gesture of his hand that I never tired of, pointing to a happy road, far away at the end of this world, and tapping the floor with his heel.

At once I was sure the patients were going to eat him alive. The nearest ones tried to reach him when he came down from the little platform. Those in the back pushed at the front ranks, trying to touch him too. A woman patient caught him by the arm and held him for a moment to her breast. Another pulled him away from her and kissed him. They all wanted to take possession of the wonder child, to take him alive, to prevent him at all costs from leaving them.

Nil, who had, without recognizing it, eased so much sadness, took fright at the terrible happiness he had unleashed. His eyes, filled with terror, called to me for help. A guard gently extricated him from the embrace of a sobbing patient:

"Dear child, little nightingale, stay here, stay here with us!"

Toward the back of the room another claimed possession of him, weeping:

50

"This is my little boy that they stole. Long ago. Give him back. Give me back my life."

He was all trembling when I got him in my arms.

"There, there, it's all finished! You made them too happy, that's all. Too happy!"

We had left the taxi, walking the rest of the way to Nil's house. He seemed to have forgotten the troublesome scene in the hospital, and his first care was to guide me, for as soon as we left the sidewalk I had no idea where I was going.

It was early May. It had rained hard for several days and the fields across which Nil was leading me were a sea of mud, with occasional clumps of low, thorny bushes that caught at my clothing. I could only guess at this strange landscape, for there were no street-lamps here. Not even what you could call a road. Just a vague path where trodden mud made the footing a little more firm than elsewhere. The path wound from one cabin to the next, and the feeble light from windows helped us somewhat. But Nil seemed not to need the light, for he jumped sure-footedly from one fairly dry spot to the next. Then we stood on the edge of a stretch of soft mud that gave off water like a sponge. To cross it there was a walk of planks thrown zig-zag here and there. The gaps were always longer than a single step. Nil would leap across and turn around to give me his hand, encouraging me to spring. He was delighted to bring me to his home; there was not a hint of suspicion in this happy child that I might pity him for living in this zone of the disinherited. It was true that beneath that soaring sky filled with stars, these cabins with their backs to the city, looking out over the free prairie vastness, formed a strangely fascinating shantytown.

From time to time, a fetid smell wafted toward us in waves, spoiling the fresh spring air. I asked Nil where it

51

came from, and at first he didn't know what I was talking about, I suppose because the smell was so familiar to him. Then he pointed behind us to a long, dark mass that blocked the horizon.

"The slaughterhouse," he said. "It must be the slaughterhouse that stinks."

Now we had crossed the muddy sea and I was fated that night to go from one surprise to the next, for the unpleasant smell suddenly gave way to the good, simple one of wet earth. Then the perfume of a flower reached me. We were coming close to Nil's house, and this was the powerful odour of a hyacinth in its pot outside near the door, struggling with a force almost equal to the last waves from the abattoir. Another few paces and the hyacinth had won. At the same time, from a nearby pond came a triumphant chorus of hylas.

Paraskovia Galaïda must have been on the lookout for us. She came at a run out of their cabin which was itself, no doubt, made of old bits of plank and waste boards. In the light of a crescent moon filtering through the clouds it seemed to me amazingly pale, as clean and pleasant as if it had just been whitewashed. It stood in a fenced enclosure. A gate opened inwards. So far as I could judge, it was made of nothing less than the foot of an iron bedstead mounted on hinges in the post. They squeaked as Paraskovia Galaïda opened the gate and welcomed us into the perfumed dooryard. The strange light revealed that everything in the place was scrupulously clean.

Paraskovia took my hands and backed toward the house. In front was a rough wooden bench. She made me sit down between Nil and herself. At once the cat of the place left the shadows and leapt to the back of the bench, where he made his narrow bed, content to be one of us, his head between our shoulders, purring.

With Nil's help, I tried to express to Paraskovia Galaïda something of the joy her small son's singing had brought

52

to so many people; and she, with his help, tried to thank me for I wasn't quite sure what. Soon we had given up trying to pour out our feelings by means of words, listening instead to the night.

Then it seemed to me I caught a sign from Paraskovia Galaïda to Nil. Her eyes closed, she gave him a starting note just as he gave it at school. A delicate musical throat vibration sounded. Their voices began together, one a little hesitant at first but quickly convinced by the stronger of the two. Then they flew upward, harmonizing as they rose in a strangely lovely song, one of life as it is lived and life as it is dreamed.

Under that immense sky it took your heart and turned it round and turned it over, as a hand might do, before leaving it an instant, with due gentleness, to the freedom of the air.

On days when all went well
during recess in the big schoolyard, with the children playing softball or prisoners' base, riding the swings or simply
running free, it might happen that the six of us who taught
the junior classes would take a stroll, three facing forward
and three walking backwards, all together, until we
reached the end of the yard, at which point we reversed the
process and started back, treating each other to little jokes
and retorts on the way, enjoying ourselves almost as much
as our pupils.

Supervision was easy on those days. The good humour
of the children really made it unnecessary. Those minutes
were a pure joy. And no doubt to anyone stopping on the
sidewalk to watch us through the steel mesh of the high
fence, our world would have seemed a life apart, protected, spared from all ills, a gage of happy tomorrows.
And no doubt it was, to a degree; but it also gave us hints
at times of misfortunes to come, of flaws deposited in innocent young lives by sinister heredities.

Three facing forward, three walking backwards, but
with serious faces this time, we were discussing this very

55

question, and the so-frequent impossibility of doing anything about the evil or unhappiness accumulated in a single creature; for Anna had bitterly complained:

"I really don't know what to do about my Demetrioff. For three months now he's been stubborn as an ox, just sits there with his arms folded."

"That's nothing," said Léonie. "Mine unfolded his, and since then he's been pounding all the others."

"How old is your Demetrioff?" said Anna.

"Eleven."

"Mine's only ten," Anna said, "but you can see sixty years of slyness and stupid stubbornness in his face." She turned to Gertrude: "What's your Demetrioff like, by the way?"

"Like a Demetrioff, what do you expect? He's only eight but already a Demetrioff to his fingertips. By the way, do yours bite theirs to the quick as well? And will you tell me where they get that dark skin, and that smell . . . that smell that stinks up the whole classroom?"

"From old Demetrioff's tannery," Denise informed us. "Did you never go by that way, in their little bit of a street – if you can call it a street! The smell gets to you five minutes away, it's enough to make you choke. The tannery's a dark sort of hole where you can hear water moving and you see the Demetrioff kids, black as demons, working away and their father cursing at them. The mother, now, is always standing still in the doorway of the cabin beside it, and she seems clean enough. That's why I think the Demetrioffs wash more than you'd think, but what good does it do? Two minutes later the smell is in their hair and on their skin again. I wouldn't be surprised if that colour comes from the water where they soak the hides."

"One thing is sure," Gertrude said, "if you've seen one Demetrioff you've seen them all. There are two or three bigger ones hanging on in the Brothers' classes. Maybe sixteen or seventeen years old. Put one of the little ones beside them and it's the same face but not quite as tough. I never saw children come out of the mould as much alike as those in every way."

"Do they get through their year?" I asked.

They all looked at me, astonished that I should even ask.

"There's not one Demetrioff," Léonie informed me, "who ever passed his year. When a teacher's had one of them the second year in a row she just pushes a little: she gives him fifty percent and away he goes to the next class up. The principal looks the other way. He knows there's nothing else to do."

"Don't they learn anything?"

"Hardly."

"Why? Are they dense?"

"No, I can't say they're dense," said Léonie. "But in the first place they come here speaking Russian – some kind of Russian. Then, the father keeps them working at home for weeks when it suits him, and then sends them back to school with a kick in the behind. No, they're not stupid, but stubborn as mules, and doing all they can, so it seems, to prove to the old man that they're not fit for school."

"They learn something, just the same," said Denise. "Brother Henry has the second or third of the big ones, and he insists he can read and write when he takes the notion."

I was stunned, I, a young teacher in my first years of work, to hear them talking about so many Demetrioffs.

"Would you please tell me how many of them there are in this school?" I asked.

"How many Demetrioffs?"

Léonie concentrated.

"All I know is, I'm on my fifth. Yes, my dears, my fifth Demetrioff, and the principal says I ought to get a medal. There are one or two of the older ones that I didn't have. And there are smaller ones to come along one of these days. How many altogether? Does anybody know how

57

many Demetrioffs there really are?"

In that moment a strange silence fell and my companions stared at me incredulously as they realized at once that I had no Demetrioff.

"No Demetrioff!"

The exclamation exploded in five different tones, including that of resentment that I was the only one to be spared.

Finally Léonie summed the situation up sensibly:

"Well, I suppose the machine had to stop sometime."

"But why for her?" complained Gertrude, pointing at me. She couldn't get over it.

But Anna was still nervous and tense. Young and enthusiastic, she would have thought herself much to blame if she didn't succeed in passing all her pupils.

"I've tried everything," she said, discouraged. "I think there's nothing for it but writing to the father, and have him in. . . ."

"Get old Demetrioff in! That's the worst thing. . . ." Léonie began to protest.

But the bell rang, and we had to take our places at the head of each class.

I wonder if the terrible consequences of Anna's idea could have been avoided if she'd had time to listen to Léonie's good advice! I'm not sure. Anna, new to life and teaching, still believed firmly that most difficulties can be solved with words. Léonie, with more experience, maintained that it was often best to let sleeping dogs lie.

In any case, waking the sleeping beast was exactly what Anna had succeeded in doing. Next day we didn't see her at recess. We heard that she was suffering from nervous shock. All sorts of rumours were doing the rounds of the school. The police, called in by the principal, were supposed to have come to take note of the injuries inflicted by Demetrioff senior on Demetrioff junior. They said Anna

58

herself had taken a fisticuff to her jaw while trying to separate the two.

It was only two days later, when Anna returned pale and shaken, that she was able to give us the true account of what had happened.

She had in fact written to old Demetrioff asking him to drop in at the school to talk about Ivan, as the boy was giving her some trouble. To be sure that the letter would reach its destination she had given it to the Demetrioff in the next class, Igor, instructing him to give it directly to his father. She could count on his doing so, for the brothers, trained in treachery, tended to exercise it on each other. We knew this, and wondered how Anna could have resorted to this extremity, and she admitted to us that when the letter was on its way she had been full of apprehension, despite the fact that she still believed in the virtue of having things out face-to-face.

Early that morning, just as she was finishing writing the day's grammar lesson on the blackboard, she had felt behind her such an unaccustomed silence that she turned suddenly toward the class. Ivan, his arms unfolded, was staring at the glass panel in the door and the face that had just appeared there. His own face was the picture of a nameless terror.

He had grown pale, said Anna. "You know how the Demetrioffs are such a dark brown you can't tell if it's their real colour or the stuff they use to treat the leather." In any case, a pallor that came from deep beneath the skin succeeded in penetrating its brown surface and showing especially around the nose, which was pinched with fright.

This sight shook her resolve to the point of making her wish she could send the visitor away. But how? After a brief blow with his knuckles on the door he had come in without waiting for a reply.

Anna told us:

"You could tell who he was a mile away! The very

mould of all our Demetrioffs. A small, shrivelled creature, his eyes no more than slits in the dark mask of his face, but so bright and cruel and piercing that you were intimidated. And if you think his children smelled of the tannery, you should have had a whiff of the father. And yet he was clean, and he had on a suit that looked quite respectable. I think he even had on a tie and I'm not sure he wasn't carrying a hat in his hand. What I know for sure, he was waving my letter in the other hand. He spread it out on my desk so that I could see it perfectly, as if I were not the one who wrote it. From the way he was bluffing I could see that he didn't know how to read. But someone must have shown him the important part, for he pointed with one of his stained, crooked fingers at the four words, 'Ivan gives me trouble.'

" 'So!' he asked, 'Ivan is trouble?'

"It was no use trying to back down or make less of Ivan's wrongdoing, or even deny it completely – the little man paralyzed me with his beady eyes and didn't give up until he had me cornered:

" 'Did you write, did you not write: Ivan is trouble?'

"I nodded my head the least bit.

" 'A little. Just a little trouble.'

" 'So!' that man shouted, and stopped listening to me.

"He turned to the class and called to Ivan.

" 'Come here, you . . . trouble!' "

Anna needed time to reassemble what had followed, bit by bit, for events had developed in a sequence akin to madness. The child, called up by his father, had come, apparently unable to look around for help. The father had taken him by an ear and hurled him against the wall. The boy bounced back only to again encounter his father, who once more sent him flying against the wall.

Ivan didn't protest or try to defend himself. Soon his mouth and nose were bleeding. Anna had tried to intervene. With one blow Demetrioff sent her about her business. Then she sent a child to fetch the principal. Even the arrival of the Brother, so impressive in his frock coat and immaculate shirtfront, hadn't the least effect on Demetrioff. He probably didn't even know whom he was up against in the distinguished person of our director. He pushed him off with the back of his hand, as he had done to Anna. And went on, taking Ivan by the same ear, now almost torn off, and hurling him against the wall. Then calmly the principal ordered the class to stand and come up *en masse* between Ivan and his father. When the man saw himself confronted by all those children, separating him from his son, he lost his certainty at once. He was as quickly deflated as he had been crafty and sudden in his attack.

"That was amazing," said Anna. "All that was left was a squat little man, as inoffensive as could be, a poor, black cinder of a thing, all the fire extinguished in his hard, little eyes."

The principal put his hand on his shoulder and Demetrioff senior followed him docilely. It was his turn to submit. The police, accompanied by a doctor, came to examine Ivan's wounds. The child was taken to the hospital and his father to the place we used for a jail in the basement of the town hall. The magistrate who tried his case was in favour of a hard sentence: three months. But who was going to look after the needs of the Demetrioff tribe for that length of time? The mother, impassive as ever, testified in her husband's favour. To her knowledge he had never punished his children beyond what they deserved. That was her message, as it arrived through the interpreter. Ivan himself, terrorized or numbed, maintained that this was the first time his father had struck so hard. That was how it went.

The father went back to his tannery and worked twice as hard to make up for lost time. Ivan returned to school with a big dressing on his ear. You'd have thought, Anna said, that nothing had happened, except that Ivan didn't fold his arms anymore.

"Apart from that," she said, "I have a feeling he's going to get back at his father. He'll be more determined than ever not to learn a thing."

Springtime came. The joy the children felt at its arrival made us gradually forget the horrible details of this affair. Then one warm and gentle day in May, during a recess loud as a beehive with laughter and shouting, we were taking our walk, three facing the front and three in reverse, when Gertrude said gaily:

"Do you know what? My Demetrioff is all rigged out brand-new today! From head to foot! Pants, shoes and even a fine wool sweater, bright red!"

"Hey! Mine has a bright-red sweater on, too!" said Denise.

"And mine!" said Solange.

"That's how it always goes," Léonie informed us. "If old Demetrioff leaves his tannery for a day it's not to outfit one child, it has to be the whole gang. And they all get the same thing so there's no time wasted! The mother has nothing to do with it. She never has a cent in her pocket. The man looks after the pennies. When the time comes he buys by the dozen or more in Eaton's basement."

"Yes, but don't you think picking flaming red shows a touch of feeling?" Gertrude asked.

We were all looking at the performing troop of children. No doubt about it, the bright red of the sweaters stood out as if a central light had scattered to different points of the yard. It went extremely well, one had to admit, with the Demetrioffs' piercing black eyes, their fringes of black hair and their tanned faces. They seemed, moreover, to have been enlivened by their new get-up, for they took more part than usual in the games, running and jumping, and we

62

had the impression of seeing an endless multiplication of flashing red sweaters!

"Didn't you see Eaton's ad this week? There was a sale of sweaters for boys from five to eighteen," Léonie told us with a touch of malice.

Gertrude protested: "Do you think there weren't awful colours there as well? He could have picked dull brown or grey – most unbecoming to our Demetrioffs!"

Toward the end of May that same year I took notion one evening to go for a walk over in what we called "Little Russia." In fact there were more Poles and Ukrainians there than real Russians, who were never very numerous in our parts. Thus they were likely even more lonely than other immigrants, who at least joined together in considerable numbers to share their exile.

Two or three times on fine evenings, I had already started out wandering in that direction but had always turned back, for Little Russia was quite far away, and my curiosity, I suppose, wasn't strong enough to keep me going. This time I persevered. At one moment, I don't know exactly when, I felt that I had crossed into unknown territory, that I had passed a frontier. For one thing, the houses no longer stood at a uniform distance from one another. They didn't even hang together in such a way as to constitute a real street. They were scattered any place, anyhow, across the fields, poor houses with their doors so low you had to stoop to go through. Tiny as they were, they were flanked by so many lean-tos, extensions, shanties, sheds and hutches that each of these wretched installations constituted a kind of little village which seemed to want to do without the others: for in all their misery they had managed to turn away from each other. I had never felt, in my own town, that I had ventured so far into foreign territory. But I was not long deceived: *I* was the foreigner here. Behind the windows hands moved, and faces on watch behind the curtains followed me with astonished, sometimes hostile stares. What was this Canadian girl doing here, in these Polish or Russian enclaves?

I went on. A wide, abandoned field lay ahead, a slice of town returned to the country, or a piece of country that had never become town, such as one sees at times, resisting for years the city that surrounds it. All the weeds of the prairie were there, even some tumbleweed looking for all the world like tangled rolls of old barbed wire. At that time of year the weeds were obviously in their winter state, with rusty leaf-blades, tall, dead grasses, and strange flowers from the preceding summer. A sad wind haunted this naked field. It seemed not to belong here but to have come with people from far away to help them keep their history more or less alive.

From afar I recognized the abominable smell that Anna had described. It was sickening. Now I could see the tannery near a curve in the river and beyond the field of weeds, encircled by low bushes. It was a shaky hut made of planks, built on piles half on the bank and half in the water of the river, whose murmur must fill it from below. Supplied at one end with already filthy water for treating the leather, the hut rejected it at the other end, barely darker in colour; and all the time the planks trembled as if they were about to float off once and for all with this brownish stream. In the doorway of a cabin close by stood a woman, her bare arms folded across her breast, a white kerchief tied beneath her chin, looking so like those one saw on the covers of popular editions of Russian novels that I wanted to touch her to make sure she was not painted. Still motionless, she granted me a brief look that I would have had trouble defining as friendly or merely curious, then she disappeared inside.

I stood alone on the threshold of the trembling tannery for a long time, trying to see in the dark interior. Light seemed to come from only one other opening on the river side, opposite the doorway where I stood; so that it crossed from one side of the shack to the other in a thin beam of sunshine. The rest of the interior remained in a dusk through which I could see the silhouettes of what looked like a horde of busy children.

Suddenly, in the middle of the lighted corridor, his black head showing in the sun like a face from an icon with its gilded halo, there appeared a little boy, so astounded at the sight of me that he was rooted to the spot. There was no mistaking him, even if he had not been wearing his red sweater. He was a Demetrioff. His eyes dark and slitted, his cheekbones high, his ears sticking out, he was the image of all the others I had seen in the schoolyard but even more puny and ill-fed, perhaps more timid. I thought he must be five and a half, perhaps six years old. He seemed unable either to take his eyes off me or to flee, so stunned was he by my sudden appearance in the tannery doorway. As for me, I was so upset by the discovery that there was another Demetrioff, and that I would likely inherit him in September, that I was as unable to stir as he. We stared at each other, the child and I, in the kind of stupor provoked by certain meetings that seem brought about by fate.

Then, suddenly, in the midst of this profoundly silent stare, a word in Russian, a word of warning, no doubt, crackled somewhere in the back of the hut, was picked up and repeated again and again in a tone of urgency, and I knew that I had been spotted. Then arms appeared from out of the shadows, seized the small Demetrioff and hauled him to safety. The last picture I have of him is that of a face convulsed with fright, unable even to utter the cry of terror I inspired in him.

Now, from the dark corner where they huddled together, came again the same word that had shaken me so, accompanied by others. I imagined that the bigger Demetrioffs, wishing to calm their little brother, were trying just as hard to indoctrinate him with a healthy fear of me. One word that kept resounding seemed particularly unpleasant. I supposed they were telling the poor child that one day I would come back for him and that day he would not be able to escape my long arm. If they seemed to love the youngest more than each other, it was clearly not with a comforting affection.

The worst thing was that I could not leave, inhibited by the very hostility from which I wanted to escape. I stood in the doorway like a bump on a log, while hissing whispers from inside seemed to let me know that I should go, that I had no business here, that the time for kidnapping the Demetrioff nestling had not yet come.

Then, two steps in front of me in the lighted zone, Demetrioff senior appeared, and with a cutting gesture put an end to the hostile chattering behind him. He was wearing a tanner's apron; his hands were the colour of stubborn rust; and his moustache was stained with the same dye. The only pale thing about him was the white around the black marbles of his pupils. The unpleasant greetings of his children had no doubt informed him as to who I was. He looked at me in silence out of his small, hard eyes, from under eyebrows that lay black and level.

I took the initiative. I counted on my fingers, listing insofar as I could the names of his children: Leonid . . . Sacha . . . Igor . . . Dmitri . . . Yuri. . . . Then I made a gesture meaning a smaller child than those. Finally I pretended to cradle a baby in my arms.

Father Demetrioff understood what I was getting at. He pointed to the little one I had just seen in the ray of sunshine, who was now coming closer again from behind, though still in the shadow, to hear what we were saying about him. Demetrioff replied:

"Yes. Him last Demetrioff."

Who could tell whether it was said with a touch of regret, or grief, or with extreme relief.

"Yes, him last," he repeated, and was moved only, it appeared, by the vibration of the floor from the streaming river. God knows how I came to the notion of taking my leave of father Demetrioff – standing stiff in the doorway – in the Orthodox manner I had seen during the Russian Easter: a slow and respectful bowing of the head and upper body, hand clasped in front. To my great surprise he returned my salute precisely, also bowing from the waist. As he straightened, his beady eyes caught mine, and I thought I saw the glimmer – though a fleeting one – of an expression slightly less distant, perhaps even one of curiosity.

On the way back to what we called "our" town and "our" life, from which I seemed to have been gone for years, I couldn't forget the picture of that little Demetrioff as he appeared to me projected against a ray of sunshine. As if to put an end to the feeling of being in a dream, I said aloud:

"So! You're going to have your Demetrioff as well!"

And I didn't know whether to be glad or sorry that I too would have a role in the dark drama that for years had placed the school and the Demetrioffs at loggerheads.

M y little Demetrioff was no more and no less alert than his brothers. Here and there he did grasp bits of lessons which he seemed, however, to have forgotten by the next morning. "That's normal for a Demetrioff," Léonie tried to encourage me. "The Demetrioffs always forget today what they learned yesterday. But sometimes part of it floats back to them, like a dream. Don't despair. All is not always lost with them."

I had, nonetheless, little hope of seeing my Demetrioff

67

make his year in a single try. I was bitterly resentful at having to pass where others had been before me.

But who would then have predicted in this sluggish child a gift so rare that it never had its equal in the history of our school!

One day I had sent some fifteen pupils to the board to practise my model *m* between lines drawn in advance. I began with this letter, which the children liked because I made it appear to them as three little connected mountains marching away together beyond the horizon. Perhaps they also liked the fact that it was the first letter of "moo-moo-moo, the call of the cow that gives good milk."

As they worked away I made my rounds, finding corrections needed almost everywhere. It was astounding how many children wrote their *m* upside down in a series of *u*'s. Others turned it into something illegible. I came to my little Demetrioff. Chalk in hand, he at last seemed happy to be in school. At least as much as any other pupil. I inspected his letters. They were perfect, of uniform height, of equal proportions, with a little tilt that made them seem to be rolling off the edge of the blackboard towards the world's end. I couldn't get over it. And the proof that he had a most exceptional hand was that where the lines stopped he had gone on, as if nothing were easier, with a row of letters just as straight and well-balanced as before. In fact he was so carried away that when his section of the board was full he had continued in his neighbour's area, with no objection from the latter, who saw this tedious work being done for him.

I congratulated my little Demetrioff by putting my hand gently on his shoulder – the only gesture of encouragement I dared to use, for he was still fearful and ready to interpret any sudden move as the beginning of a blow. He looked up at me with a gaze that hesitated between fear and a feeble ray of hope, which grew as he saw I was pleased with him. Then seeing that this was all he had to do to please me, he

68

took up his chalk again and continued the march of letters as if he had never done anything else all his life. The other children made room for him, as it was clear he was out to fill the board. They were a little dazzled too by such virtuosity.

I took Demetrioff's chalk and made him a sample capital *M*. He was a strange child. When he understood, he didn't smile as almost any child would do in his pleasure at grasping an abstract idea. All that happened was, the small black marbles of his eyes acquired a tiny, additional glint. He stood on tiptoe, took the chalk from me and made an *M* that was just as good as mine, if not better. I took the chalk again and made a specially fancy letter with curlicues and flourishes on all sides. I had barely finished when he stretched again to take the chalk. Biting his lip in concentration, trembling with the tension of his effort, he made the letter and handed me the chalk with the mute vivacity of a little dog who brings back a stick to his master and seems to beg, "Once more, and farther!"

I was less enchanted when I discovered that Demetrioff the Last had not the slightest idea what the letter was that he had formed so well in small and capital versions.

I dug out a picture of a mooing cow. I went *moo, moo, moo*. The rest of the class, exasperated at seeing this dull business go on and on, started making horns at each other, their fingers sticking out from their heads. They were all mooing at once. The poor child, looking blank, realized that something had to do with a cow – but what was she doing in the school, and what in the world could be the connection between this animal and the graceful letter he had learned to make so perfectly? Finally, from a long way off, a kind of comprehension struck his mind. A brief glimmer showed in his opaque gaze. His passion apparently lay not in knowing his letters, just in copying them. It was then I thought I might have found a way to give him an incentive to learn.

Until he had recognized and pronounced aloud the first letters of the words I proposed – *p*, for example – and learned them by heart, he would not be allowed to write them on the board.

The poor child was in a sweat. His hair damp at his temples, he would search the eyes of other children to find out how they managed to understand. And when he succeeded, it seemed that it was by a kind of mimesis, a curious power of osmosis, the others' ability reaching him through a communion of knowledge. Then, having finally won the right to go to the blackboard, which seemed to be his life's aim, he kept repeating the lesson he had just learned so as not to forget it, and you could hear him whispering puh-puh-puh while his little hand gave birth to letters that seemed to dance in their new-found freedom.

There were days when to reward him I let him write to his heart's content. One afternoon when I had almost forgotten him, he spent more than an hour at the board. When I turned to see what he'd been doing all that time, I almost fell over with astonishment. He had written the whole alphabet, small letters and capitals, with not a single mistake in their order. Where on earth had he learned so much that he was far ahead of my lessons? Had his brothers, proud of his gift, helped him along at home? Or was it possible that he had remembered all the letters at once, and on his own?

I looked at him in silence. His exploit ended – it stretched along the full length of the blackboard – he was exhausted, smiling vaguely through an enormous weariness. But what was it, anyway, this passion that ruled him? With his strange eyes, their dark fire turned inward, his face captivated rather than transfigured, he reminded me of those little anonymous saints on the iconostases of the Greek Church, who adore their creator from afar without dreaming of asking him to cast his eye upon them.

I noticed too that he assumed almost an attitude of

prayer when, after writing his letters, he gave himself a moment to contemplate them. What was this story he was writing without the need to read it in order to understand?

Slowly I came to the notion that he himself was not the moving spirit in his dogged determination to write. Perhaps it was a distant hunger. A long, mysterious wait. I had the impression that this poor child was impelled to write by generations long past, exerting on him their most pitiless pressure.

Parents' day was approaching. We used to invite them to sit in on our classes, spending part of the day at school, to help them realize what it meant to teach their children. My Demetrioff was beginning to understand a few non-Russian words. I told him it would be very good if his father could come to see for himself how well his little boy could write.

To tell the truth, we teachers found it a killing day, with our classrooms invaded by parents who didn't know what to do with themselves. It was no use putting chairs at the back of the room; they wouldn't stay there. On pins and needles at the discovery that their child was not as brilliant as they might have thought, they would have given anything to be able to prompt. Some were upset beyond measure at seeing their offspring in a light other than that of home. Some, it's true, had pleasant surprises, and told us on the verge of tears: "I'd never have thought my little tad was so smart!"

For us, the teachers, it meant playing to the gallery. For on a day like that, who would be so simple-minded as to ask questions of the dullard pupils and ignore the stars?

Around ten o'clock, under the scrutiny of a dozen women – it was mostly the mothers who came – I was trimming my sails as best I could: Don't let the sewerman's son show up too well; be sure the police-chief's son gets the right question, his mother's rolling her eyes already; but also let it be seen that justice is done. . . . The door opened with a bang and Demetrioff senior came in, and with him the smell of his tannery. But apart from that, he was clean, his cheeks scrubbed until they shone like waxed leather, and in his heavy, brick-red hands he was twisting a brand-new cap.

With his little weasel eyes he took in the classroom and its visitors, then went to the back and took up his position, standing among the poorer parents who, in their excessive shyness, made me most shy. At once he spotted his son in the middle of the class and from that moment hardly took his eyes off him.

The child, ill-at-ease beneath this stare, did not feel free to avoid it, and responded continually with his own frightened glance. Yet a current was passing between them. Of defiance, of hope, of fear? It would have been hard to define the secret tension. I just hope, I thought, that my young Demetrioff isn't entirely put off by it. In fact, if I had invited the father it was because I felt certain he would never again set foot in the school after last year's scandal. His presence left me flustered. I couldn't help looking his way out of the corner of an eye, and I was so uneasy that at times I didn't know what I was doing. Standing there with his cap in his hand, he looked harmless enough; but Anna too had at first taken him for good-natured.

Suddenly I felt I couldn't keep it up. It wasn't in writing or arithmetic that my poor little Demetrioff was going to shine. He never raised his hand to answer the questions I asked. Demetrioff senior seemed to show a growing surprise at all those hands going up while his son made not a single move. But it was always possible that he didn't understand what was happening or why the children raised their hands time after time.

I decided to pass at once to the writing lesson. I made a

little speech for the parents' benefit, explaining why a "good hand" acquired in childhood was a great advantage in later life. I also mentioned that one shouldn't learn to write with the fingers, as this was bad for the nervous system and the child's behaviour, but rather from the wrist or even from the elbow, according to the system prescribed; and also that I tried to help the children to write rhythmically by having them sing as they wrote at the board.

I sent up about half my class to write, with Demetrioff among them. They started writing and singing with gusto, because they had come to take pleasure in this lesson, with its lively music, and perhaps also because I had put so much effort into making them like it.

The parents moved closer, or, if they stayed where they were, leaned forward to get a better view of their child at work. I caught some of them making sour faces; but most smiled indulgently and two mothers nodded to each other in a complicity of mutual congratulation. Then after seeing their own children at work, they all turned to watch little Demetrioff writing.

As usual, and inexplicably as ever, he filled his square of the board starting from the bottom. Now, on tiptoe, he had reached the upper part. Absorbed in what he was doing, he seemed to have forgotten where he was, with no notion that he had become the focus of all eyes, the classroom having grown silent and attentive. He was writing, if one can use the word in this context, as though inspired. Sticking out the tip of his tongue, he was sweating a little at the temples, but at the same time he seemed carried away by a force that went beyond his own, a fervour that might have been collective, mysterious and infinite. Perhaps this was how the humble scribes of another age had written, sheltered by monasteries where they earned their bread by transcribing, beneath the gaze of pious paintings, the texts of immortal legends of which they themselves understood not a word. With his fringe of black hair over his earth-coloured face, his eyes squinting, his attitude of prayer, he made me think of those obscure and humble artisans who were at times given their modest place below the iconostasis, behind the archimandrite bedizened in his rich vestments.

Demetrioff senior approached: cautiously, as if he were afraid of scaring off a bird. In a stupor of astonishment he contemplated the letters, then the little brown hand that had made them, then the letters again.

Then – did he do it for sport? – he took the chalk from the boy and, in the space remaining at the top of the board, tried his own hand at forming a few letters. There was a little laughter in the room at the touching clumsiness of his efforts. To this laugh the man replied with a kind of friendly grunt. He returned the chalk to the child and poked him in the back to start him writing again. He needed no prompting.

Then, after a few minutes, the father took the brush, cleaned off the whole square of piously written letters and gave the child another little push in the back. Without a second's delay he started his letters all over again, with the same fervour and patience as before. What dream, in heaven's name, was he obeying?

And the father? Suddenly, as I looked deep into his dark, small eyes, I thought I caught the same strange, stubborn fervour as on the face of the child.

At the very top, isolated from the rest of the blackboard by a double line, was a border composed of the alphabet, small letters and capitals.

I had recently taken off the strip of paper with drawings of tulips in flower which I had used to hide the letters, for I thought them too fancy to serve as models but hadn't yet found the courage to erase my predecessor's careful work. Well, Demetrioff senior now put his thick finger under one of these elaborate letters and gave the child his little push,

74

and the last Demetrioff performed. The father picked another one at random, and the child reproduced it as well, but in a purer, more sober style which had something classical about it. Then the father turned toward the class. With his little shiny eyes he stared us down, forcing us to witness that beyond the shadow of a doubt Demetrioff the Last knew how to write. What the letters stood for perhaps mattered no more to him than to his son. The gift of being able to trace them was marvellous enough.

Awkwardly he took his son's shoulder. In his rough way, he dug his fingers in for a moment, trying not to be too brusque about drawing the child's head toward his arm. His son resisted, only half-confident. At last he let his fearful little face rest against his father's sleeve. He looked up at him apprehensively. Then there passed between them a smile so fleeting, so clumsy, so tentative, that it seemed the first to be exchanged between those two faces.

Part 2

The school to which I was appointed that year could, I suppose, be called a part of the village, though it hung back at the very end, separated from the last houses by a good-sized field in which a cow used to graze. Despite this gap, there was no doubt that I belonged to the village – a dreary place with its poor houses, most of them in unpainted wood, already decrepit before the last board was nailed; and its tiny chapel, built out of antagonism to the next village with its rich and fancy church. But it was out of antagonism too that the priest from the rich parish had never set foot in the little chapel, which was gradually crumbling in neglect.

From the school windows I could see the bleak railway station, like all those built at the time, with its grain elevators, its water tank, a caboose that had been sitting on the ground for years. Everything was painted in that hateful ox-blood colour that had no life or sparkle; but very likely because it was lifeless, it was durable and money-saving. The main street predominated of course, treeless and too wide, a melancholy dirt road, plaintive and dusty as the main streets of almost all the villages of the Canadian West in the first year of the Great Depression. It was a village of retired farmers, bitter or acrimonious, with barely enough to live on, old folk, homebodies, little businesses just scraping by. There was nothing in the place to give you courage or confidence or hope in any tomorrow. But I only had to turn the other way and everything changed: hope came back in giant waves; I seemed to be looking toward the future, and that future shone with the most alluring light it ever revealed in my lifetime.

Yet there wasn't anything to see. Not the roof of a house, nor a barn, not even one of those tiny granaries you found all over the prairies when the harvests were too big to sell. Just a stretch of dirt road that rose a little, turned a little, then was lost in infinity. After that, nothing but the sky, a shoulder of rich black earth against the rich blue of the horizon and, occasionally, clouds rigged like old-fashioned sailing ships. Why, in a country so young, does hope come to us from desert spaces and the marvellous silence!

It's true that more than half my pupils came from that wild side that looked so uninhabited. Until it grew too cold, toward mid-October, they all came on foot, except for a few mornings when there was heavy rain.

From the very first week, sitting at my desk, which looked out toward the plain, I got in the habit of watching them arrive. I came early to prepare my lessons. I had to: I had forty pupils divided into eight grades, from the first to the eighth year. Having so many classes was the great problem of those country schools, but it was also their incredible advantage. With children of all ages they constituted a sort of family, a world in itself. Today they'd call it a commune.

I was very often ready well before school-time, the blackboard covered with examples and problems to be solved. Then I'd sit down and start looking impatiently for my pupils to arrive. My eyes never left the lonely rise in the road where I'd see them appear one by one or in groups that sketched a little border against the sky's edge. I would see their tiny silhouettes pop up in the immensity of the empty prairie, and I felt the vulnerability, the fragility of the children of the world, and how it was, nonetheless, on their frail shoulders that we loaded the weight of our weary hopes and eternal new beginnings.

I remember how overwhelmed I was that from all directions they were converging on me, an outsider to them after all. To this day I'm still astonished and touched to think that people should entrust to a total stranger – fresh from Normal School as I was then – the most delicate, the newest, the easiest thing to break in this whole world.

Soon, even at that distance, I could tell them apart: the Badiou children, who held each other by the hand, not only on the last stretch but, as I later found out, for the whole two miles from their farm, their anxious mother having put the boy of five and a half in the care of his sister who was six and a half, and her in the care of her little brother; and they no doubt felt some protection in holding hands. The Cellinis formed a compact group, the five of them, only Yvan the terrible, Yvan the rebel, dragging behind, with Adele, the eldest, turning to make signs for him to hurry. Then there were my children from the Auvergne, who kept to themselves, never mixing with the Italians, still less with those from Brittany, easy to recognize by their slogging step; the two little Morissots who, rain or shine, late or early, I saw arriving on the run, like madmen; the Lachapelles, making a ladder on the horizon, the tallest in front, the smallest last, walking at an unchanging pace, keeping equal distances between them; and finally, almost always alone, often last of all and a few minutes late, a little silhouette that hurried, his shoulders

81

bent forward, his schoolbag on his back, seeming over-burdened.

Oh, that boy! There's still a tightening around my heart when I think of him!

His name was André Pasquier. And he wasn't a bad pupil, far from it, nor lacking in any way. But – how can I put it? – while he was hard-working, with the best will in the world, one that I could reproach with nothing in particular, he was always off somewhere. Preoccupied, you would have said. No doubt worried by some cares at home that wouldn't be shaken off. And he seemed tired even as the school day began. How could he make the effort I expected of him?

One day when I saw him struggling over a problem that the others had solved in half the time, I stopped at his desk.

"What's the matter, André? Are you tired?"

"Yes, a bit," he said, and his eyes had the wandering look that one sees in some men who are broken by physical exhaustion.

"Do you help a lot at home?"

"Oh, not that much. I have to do some. I'm the oldest. It's my job to help my father."

"Do you have far to walk?"

"It's two and a half miles."

Dear me! And I'd scolded him just yesterday for being late!

"That's quite a stroll, isn't it?"

"Oh, it's not so bad," he said, managing a smile. "The fresh air is good for you."

I helped him solve his problem – the little one of the moment – and went back to my desk. From then on this child was never far from my mind. I was determined to bring to his life, which I felt was difficult in the extreme, at least the possibility of escape through education. At all costs I wanted him to succeed in class. But how to go about

82

it? Keep him after school to go over his lessons? I'd make his day that much longer. Give him special attention in school hours? He was touchy and proud. If he noticed, he could withdraw even deeper into himself. Yet this was the only way; but I had to use the utmost discretion. After a week I had the joy of seeing him finish his work almost as soon as the others.

I congratulated him, and I hardly recognized in this child–astonished at himself, dazzled by his own performance–the poor little boy who some days came to school so tired that I'd have thought he had been drinking.

"See, André! When you try!"

And I put out my hand to pat his cheek or his forehead. And now, unlike other times, he didn't recoil, acting the little man, but allowed a fallen lock of hair to be pushed back.

It seemed to me from that day on, if he arrived late, weary, sometimes sad, that little by little in the course of the day his soul, light and tender, would surface above the worries that were too much for his age; and he would be astonished to enjoy a moment without care.

One day I heard him laugh, for the first time, at I don't know what. I was struck by this, and went to look at his notebook. There was no doubt he had made a great deal of progress.

I asked him:

"Are your parents anxious for you to get an education?"

"Oh, yes! My father says he doesn't want me to be like him, with no schooling, no trade, nothing."

I wanted to chase away the seriousness and concern that had come back in his eyes at the mention of home, and I said to the others, half laughing, half seriously:

"You just look out for André. He's a slow starter like the tortoise, but who knows if he won't come in ahead of all of you hares and rabbits!"

83

André gave me a hesitant look that had something of a man's reproachful glance: Don't push it too far, now . . . But there was also a flash of a child's wild belief in the impossible.

What had got into me, to make me put such intense hope in his head?

Of the two of us, I must have been the bigger child.

By four o'clock, full of vitality though I was in those days, I would be so weary and exhausted that I would sit idle at my desk for a long while, gathering courage to attack the pile of notebooks in front of me.

If I looked up toward the lonely little slope I could see the morning's film projected in reverse against the horizon. Now André was in the lead, his shoulders hunched forward, hurrying with the pace of a man returning to pressing duties. Then came the Lachapelles, not in single file now, but – what next! – with the bigger ones giving their hands to the smaller ones for the evening walk. Only the Badiou children never changed, morning or evening, week after week, holding hands and gracefully, tirelessly, swinging the two arms joined together. All my little people were making their way up the gentle slope, each at his own pace, in his own manner, each in turn printed for a second on the sky, which was often fiery at those early sundowns. For one instant I would see them in an aureole of light at the top of the road, then the unknown would snatch them from me.

At those times I found myself wondering about their lives on the distant farms about which I knew nothing. I suspected that an infinite distance separated their lives there from our life at school, but I was still far short of the truth: between those two lives rose a frontier that was almost insurmountable. Yet I dreamed of setting foot in those isolated farmhouses, of perhaps being accepted by those silent, sometimes hostile households. Then, miraculously, the chance was offered me by the little Badiou girl, whose mother had taught her what to say, and who came one day to say it at my desk, word for word, chirping gently like a sparrow:

"My mother, mamzelle, she says for me to say this that it would give her the greatest pleasure if you would do us the honour of having supper at our place one of these evenings at your convenience."

So as to forget no part of this solemn invitation little Lucienne had rattled it off without a pause. And even with her eyes closed.

I said, very pleased:

"Of course, Lucienne. I'd love to go with you. And why not tonight? It's such a nice day."

In fact, after one or two nights of hoar frost we were being treated to Indian summer. It was as hot as the finest day in summer; but everyone knows that these radiant days in October are an exceptional gift, to be withdrawn promptly. I felt like taking advantage of it.

The child hesitated, caught between a great satisfaction and a certain disappointment.

"It's just that mama won't have time to houseclean, or at least sweep up the worst, or even bake her cake."

And she underlined each regretful phrase with a gesture of one old gossip to another, letting her hands fall to her sides.

"She wouldn't want to not have her cake ready, at least."

"What's the difference? It's not the cake, it's the company that counts."

At four o'clock quite a few pupils were waiting for me on the front step, out of politeness, because I was going their way. We left together, but with one group within the other, so to speak, as the

Badiou children had made it clear that I belonged to them for that evening, and they had come to take my hands, Lucien on my left and Lucienne on my right, swinging them at a great rate as they did between themselves, so that in no time my arms were aching and I had to beg them to set me free. As they did so, they were no doubt surprised to find themselves free of each other, for they were off at a run, Lucien to peer and poke into a gopher hole with a stick, and Lucienne to put two or three mushrooms into her skirt. Then they came back to their places at my side, threatening any who would usurp them. They relaxed their surveillance only when it became clear that I couldn't really escape. My little Auvergnats, however, were stubbornly gaining ground.

Soon we formed a single group, if not a friendly one at least more or less united. Only André kept the lead, yet without dissociating himself from the group, for when he saw that he was getting too far ahead he would slow down, forcing himself to wait; but soon, as if he couldn't help it, he was leaving us behind with the pace of one who has never learned to take his time.

We arrived at the top of the little knoll. We stopped. Looked back. I could see myself at my desk, watching me go up to the top of the road with the children, and I was pleased with the picture that rose in my imagination. From here the school looked bigger than I had thought, and higher, with its second floor formerly occupied by another classroom when there had been more children. Its worn paint, still faintly white at this distance, stood out rather well in the dull landscape. The graceful belfry on its roof even gave it a certain refinement. For the first time I realized that, poor and all as the village was, it had put its money on the school as being an essential possession.

Then I turned and saw the prairie, that endless gulf into which my children plunged every evening. The sight did not lift my heart in joy as when I looked at it from the

86

village. Perhaps deserts, the sea, the vast plain and eternity attract us most when seen from the edges.

I grew silent. The children, finding me different from what I usually was in their eyes, were disconcerted. They looked questioningly at me, pointedly, as if they were wondering:

Is that still her? Is it?

My moment of gravity passed. It may have come from a presentiment of a sadness still hidden in the future – a thing that has happened often in my life. I was back with the children now, and as soon as they were aware of it, they came back to me, gay and confident and chattering, real little magpies. In ten minutes they told me more than I had taught them in days.

Toutant's cow had calved. They'd had a lot of trouble with her, for the calf came out wrong-way around. Jos Labossière had taken his sow to the boar. She'd have little pigs in a few months. And Mrs. Toutant had lost her baby when just on the way – months too soon.

"And you know how big a baby is, mamzelle, a baby born six months too soon? Not very big."

Lucienne tugged at my sleeve and confided:

"Mama had her baby three months ago at our place, a real one, and he's big and beautiful."

I saw that I had nothing to teach them about birth, human or animal; and both appeared to have the same importance to them.

At last we came to a house. Here the Lachapelles were going to leave us. A woman with a ponderous breast, in a dress of flowered cotton, her thick arms bare, opened the door and shouted to me from the threshold:

"Where are you leaving to go, then?"

"To the Badious."

"That's right. Go and see the French, never your own people."

"But madame!"

87

"I just said that for something to say. Will you drop in at least on the way back?"

"Of course, madame."

"A'right, then. Come on, kids. Off with the new, on with the old."

At that instant the five Lachapelles, who were quite affectionate toward me at school, became like little strangers who had never heard tell of me. If I hadn't known to what madness embarrassment can push certain children, I would have been stupefied. But I just said to the five wooden faces looking past me toward a picket fence:

"Good-bye, children, see you tomorrow!"

A little farther on, at the junction of the road and a section byway, we lost the Auvergnat children whose farmhouse was a quarter of a mile away, alone in the immensity of its fields.

Before they left us, the little girls began to lament:

"Mama's going to be really happy when she finds out you started your tour with the Badious!"

"In the first place, it isn't a tour. In the second place, if your mother wants me to visit, tell her I'd be delighted to come."

Our group continued, thinned out now. We talked less, walked more slowly, perhaps because we were a little tired; and, for my own part at least, in order to admire the landscape. In the light of the sun, which was about to disappear, it was uniformly bright in colour, drowsy and tranquil in a way that perhaps disquieted the spirit because of its infinite depth. Almost all the harvest was in the barns. What remained to cover the earth was stubble, golden in itself and tinted a fairer blond by this soft light of the day's end. Few and far between, trees reddened by autumn stood flaming in their bursts of colour. All the rest was sweetness and peace, or rather the occasional harmony found in nature as it huddles over its secret.

We crossed a long stretch of prairie without a single building, and heard no cock crow and no dog bark, nor even the wild birds of the place. André was walking with us now, his hurry appeased at least. He didn't join in the conversation but his head, a little to one side, seemed to spring up to listen after a moment's silence. In this way, we would exchange a few words, mostly about the harvest, which had been good in this place, bad in that. Then we would fall back into a vague reverie, perhaps due to the walk in the fresh air or the magic influence of the day's end on the prairie.

As the road climbed out of a slight hollow, a house became visible, still far away, surrounded by fence-posts, each of which had a milk-pail for a hat. The little Morissots began to shout with joy:

"That's our place! That's our place!"

As we approached, their mother came out to the fence to greet me with a rapid-fire monologue that never stopped. It was about me, the children, the harvest, the school, a trip to town she was about to undertake, the hard life, the good weather these days, the winter coming and God knew how we'd get through it. . . . Finally she grabbed her two children by the hands and the three went into the house, running.

Only a short way farther, Lucienne, who always pulled at my sleeve when she had something to confide, gave a great tug and said:

"You can never get a word in with her. Mama says there's not a woman alive talks more than Madame Morissot."

"Maybe she's bored, alone out here at the end of the world."

Lucienne put on an offended expression because it seemed I did not share her ideas completely, and went on pointedly:

"We're even more alone at our place."

I thought I saw the shadow of a smile pass over André's face, but he said nothing.

There were just four of us now. We continued on our way. The Morissots' house was soon hidden by one of the rare patches of trees in the area, and we found ourselves again penetrating what seemed to be the earth's hidden face.

"The sun is dead!" Lucien suddenly cried in a plaintive voice. He had been watching its descent below the horizon, and came to press against me, trembling with sadness.

I could now imagine what these tots must feel as they went through the small wood – which to them might seem like a forest – at the moment the sun was setting.

To me this hour that hesitates between night and day has always seemed enchanted. It always called to me; it calls me still like a dream in which our torments will be stilled. It has happened that without realizing it I would walk for two hours in a row under the darkening sky toward the last flush of the horizon, as if it held for me the answer to the question that haunts us from birth. And that evening – so young then and even more than now given to dreaming – I crossed through that hour of sweetness, holding the hands of Lucien and Lucienne to reassure them, with André just a shade ahead. And it seemed to me that we were climbing infallibly, the three children and I, toward happiness, still out of sight but certain to be waiting for us before too long. Emerging from a hollow we were struck by a last arrow of light darting from the horizon. André received it full in his face, and I discovered with astonishment the strange and splendid colour of his eyes: a spring leaf traversed by sunlight.

Silence still enveloped us, not oppressively as when it signifies the absence of life but swollen with a happy revelation on the point of being made. And then in the golden stubble we heard a burst of bubbling song in the distance. I stopped the children with a gesture and laid my other hand on André's shoulder. "Listen! Wait just a moment, we'll hear the meadowlark!"

Lucien and Lucienne pretended to listen, looking all over to find the bird; but André listened from within, his head tilted, not caring from what point might come such an expression of joy that perhaps no one has sung it better than this bird – yet a queer solitary figure when we came upon him at last, sitting on a stone in a bare field.

When the song ended, André turned his eyes toward mine, and I saw a delight that was equal to my own.

After that the road was level for a long time. The blue of evening grew darker all around until all shapes were imprecise. The Badious started pointing somewhere in the great emptiness.

"We're home! That's our place!"

Finally I was able to make out a poor, colourless cabin, no porch, just a cube fallen there like dice on a table.

The Badiou children were pulling me along with all their strength, announcing with loud cries that carried far through the infinite silence:

"Mama! Mama! We've brought our mamzelle!"

Much in the same way, it seemed to me, they might have boasted: We've caught her!

Then, out of the little house that stood at the end of a faint trace of laneway, came a small, round woman, agile and agitated, lively as a weasel. When she knew who I was she began to flap her arms at her sides and in the same breath cried that I was so nice to have come . . . and then, abashed: "My house is a mess! And my kitchen's not scrubbed!"

I later understood that it was better manners to give people some time to make special preparations for your visit. But it seemed in this case that the joyous exuberance of this little woman was stronger than her shame at being caught in her "old rags" with the house "all upside-down."

91

On the point of going inside, I looked back to the road. André was already moving on. Now in the gathering dusk he seemed terribly alone. His shoulders had sunk forward again.

"Hey! André!"

He turned.

"Have you far to go?"

He pointed in the direction of a kind of combe from which emerged a few large, black treetops and, among them, the roof of a house that seemed uninhabited. In that direction everything seemed darker than elsewhere on the plain. You'd have said that was where the night came from.

"How far is it still?"

"Half a mile," he said. "That's why I have to hurry now."

He stood there, unmoving for a moment, not saying a word, as if he regretted not having the right, like other children, to say to me: You'll come to my place one of these days. . . .

He simply made a curious despairing gesture with his arms.

"Well, good night, André. See you tomorrow!"

"Good night, mamzelle!"

As I watched him go, almost at a run, I never dreamed how little I was to see of him in the future.

Less than two weeks after that walk under the Indian summer sky, the icy rains came, and piercing winds; and then – just on the first of November – we woke up to find the poor prairie village surrounded by dunes of snow, like a desert fort amid the sands.

As I kept watch over the little slope that morning, I had the pleasure of seeing, instead of small silhouettes with shoulders hunched, a whole series of cutters. First came Cellini, a man in a hurry, who stopped in for a minute to warm his big hands over the register, telling me that from now on he would bring his children to school and pick them up at four o'clock sharp, and let's be clear about it, he wouldn't wait for anyone who had a detention, let them walk home, it would serve them right. Then came Odilon Lachapelle, in such a rush to leave that the last child barely had one foot out of the cutter and he was on his way home. Then an enormous man with a moustache, with the little troop of Auvergnats cuddled around him under the same buffalo robe. And finally Morissot, who also brought the Badiou children. When I saw that, I wondered why they hadn't all thought of asking him, or one of the parents, to gather all the children from that side of the world and pay him a little for his trouble, rather than have each family underway with the sleds. Everybody would have gained. But apparently our people weren't ready to think that way, at least in those days.

While the children, happy that they didn't have to walk, were hanging up their coats and chattering gaily, a pleasant smell of cold and snow spread through the room, tempered by the waves of heat from the stove.

I rejoiced with them. Now they would start their day rested, good-humoured, and everything would go much better. Then I noticed that André was missing. I asked the Badious, the Morissots:

"You didn't see him on the way?"

"No."

He didn't arrive until about one hour later, walking, his cheeks burning with the cold, and he was still shaking with it after he'd stood over the register a good five minutes. Again he had trouble concentrating on his grammar and geography and arithmetic. And it seemed to me, as I looked at this exhausted child, that those subjects weren't worth making such a fuss about. He came to my desk to show me his notebook, and I took the opportunity to say to him, almost in a whisper:

93

"Won't your father be driving you to school too, very soon?"

"Not a chance!" he said. "He's already got too much to do in the mornings, all the chores, feeding, milking. . . ."

"But couldn't you make some arrangement with the Badious or the Morissots? You could walk to their place and they'd bring you from there."

He put his shoulders back.

"We don't like being obliged. They'd have to wait if I wasn't on time. And they don't always leave at the same time every day. No, we thought about it, but it's too much to ask."

"Well! At least your father's going to pick you up in the afternoon! It gets dark so early now."

In his eyes, which were not so much sad as resigned, those of a man who has seen it all, there passed an expression of annoyance . . . perhaps because I was poking my nose into his life with such persistence.

"It's the same thing at night," he explained, but still politely, as if our roles were reversed and I was the child whose eyes had to be opened to hard realities. "It's the livestock, the chores, the milking. And our horse couldn't do it. He's all we have in winter. And he has to go a mile and a half twice a day for water. It's hard in this weather. You have to break the ice. My father's tired out when he comes back the second time. . . . You can't ask too much," he said with pity.

"Of course, André. I didn't know all those things. But at least you could go home at night with the Badious. You'd only have another half-mile to walk. Do you want me to ask for you?"

He seemed hesitant, torn between his secretive nature and the confidence I had been able to inspire in him. Lifting his arms as if to say, what can you do? – he finally murmured:

"It's not worth it, mamzelle."

94

"What do you mean, it's not worth it?"

His lips trembled.

"Oh, well. I didn't want to tell you just now. Mama said to wait a week or two yet and get what I can out of it. But I know there's no other way. I'm going to quit school, mamzelle."

"Leave school! André! You musn't think of it!"

He lifted his arms again, like a pair of powerless wings.

"My father can't get on alone. And where does it get him, working like a horse? He's going to a logging shanty up north. He'll earn enough there to keep us going. So I have to keep the house."

"What about your mother?"

"She's been in bed nearly two months now."

"You didn't tell me she was ill."

"She's expecting . . ." he said briefly.

Barely getting out his words, he continued close to my ear:

"If she gets up in those times she'll likely lose her baby, and anyway she's too sick to do anything but give orders from her bed."

"Is there no one else at your place to help out?"

"Just Émile."

"Your little brother? How old is he?"

"Five."

A flash of intense pride, almost of maternal joy, lit the depths of his worried eyes.

"You'd be surprised how he can work, bringing in wood, washing dishes. . . . He's a real little helper, Émile is. At night when I have time I give him lessons. He can read already. You'll see, mamzelle, when he comes to school, he's going to be a lot smarter than I was."

His defences down, he was, for that moment, dreaming aloud of a happy furture for his little brother Émile.

"But you're only a child yourself. And far too young to keep house, come now!"

95

"I'm past ten. I'll be eleven in two months."

That afternoon I managed to get him into Guillaume Morissot's cutter, and to ask the driver in secret if he couldn't wait for André in the mornings and take him back at night.

He answered good-naturedly:

"If those folks weren't so proud, of course we'd do a favour between neighbours. But with them it ain't easy, believe me, mamzelle."

Sitting warm with the others under the robes in the sled that took off with a start, André was the only child that showed no joy. His little face with its big, worried eyes was elsewhere, already busy with the chores that awaited him. He was never to come back to school again.

Weeks and finally months passed by and I realized that not for a single day had I stopped telling myself: It can't be, he's going to come back. Nor had I given up watching the lonely rise in the road, now a high barrier of snow, in the hope of seeing again, as I had the last time, the frail silhouette with the thin, hunched shoulders. . . . And I hadn't even any news. Not a word!

I often asked the Morissots and the Badious. Had they any news?

Lucienne shrugged and flapped her arms. She said:

"Not a thing, mamzelle! They never get in touch, the Pasquiers. So we just wait. No use stickin' your nose in other people's business."

One day I met Mrs. Morissot at the general store.

"That poor woman," she said, meaning Mrs. Pasquier, "it's a downright shame, lying in bed almost all the time she's pregnant. It's her constitution, not the same as other women. We'd go and help out but it's not easy, you know.

Those people, when they get that miserable, they won't let you near them.''

At Christmas I had sent André by way of the Badious the little present which the school board allowed for every pupil. I added some candies and also sent fruit for Émile. It wasn't until the end of January that I received a note of thanks, and I supposed that the Badious had not been in too great a hurry to deliver my package. The little thank-you note was signed in André's already firm hand, and underneath, in capitals contained between two pencilled lines, Émile had put his name.

Then came February and days of startling beauty. The sun was gaining strength. One afternoon of fine weather was enough to start the surface snow melting, only to crystallize in the cold of the night, and next morning offering to the fire of the rising sun the glinting of a cut stone with a million facets. This hard crust carried well, and one Saturday morning I put on my skis and, ignoring the road, set off across the prairie toward the Pasquiers' farm.

This time seeing it first from the back, from the top of a knoll, I had no trouble finding the house in its narrow combe surrounded by leafless trees. There it squatted, along with its outbuildings, weathered by time but not ugly in shape, with the high gables stretching to capture a piece of sky above its sombre nest. And no doubt in the years when its paint was new – light yellow, so far as I could judge – it must have looked very spruce in its green background.

I glided down the slope to the back door, which seemed to be the only one in use, as was the case with many farm-houses in winter. A deep path, like a trench in the snow, led up to it. As I took off my skis I thought I heard vague sounds coming from inside, which stopped as soon as I knocked on the door. I imagined a lively commotion within, as most likely no one had seen me coming. At last I saw the doorknob turn, very slowly. The door opened a crack, revealing half the face of a child with green-gold eyes like those of André. It expressed the stupefaction of a shipwrecked sailor seeing another turn up on his island.

"So you're Émile!"

Then he opened the door and let me in without saying a single word, staring at me with intense curiosity. I was in a large, bright kitchen where washing hung from cords strung from side to side. From a room that opened off it, a weak voice called:

"Is somebody there? Who is it, Émile?"

Then Émile's voice was raised in triumph, high and shrill:

"It's the lady from the school, mama."

"Good Lord!" cried the voice, taking on a warmer tone. "Bring her in, Émile, quickly. Put a stick in the stove. Take her coat. As soon as she's warmed up a little bring her in to me."

Then she spoke directly to me, without having seen me, perhaps a little embarrassed:

"You must excuse the mess, mademoiselle. Do come in."

I went through the open bedroom door and saw, lying flat on her back on a wide iron bed, the quilt outlining her swollen belly, a woman with a beautiful face whose immense, sad but gentle eyes met mine with warm emotion.

"Quick, Émile, clear off a chair for the lady. . . . No, put those things on the chest. . . . Oh, there's dust on the table! Give it a wipe with the cloth, Émile, my dear."

And to me:

"Sit down, mademoiselle, please sit down."

As soon as I was seated near the bed, she stretched out a thin hand to seize mine and shake it, while tears ran down her cheeks. Standing in the doorway, Émile was trying to hold back his. Seeing this, she sent him away, but tenderly:

"Now then, make yourself useful, you rascal. Get up on the chair. Open the draught a bit in the stovepipe, but don't forget, as soon as the wood starts crackling climb up and turn it shut again. And while you're on the chair you can take down some of the washing. It must be almost dry. Fold it properly, now.''

When the child, busied with the stovepipe, was making enough noise to cover our voices, she made her excuses to me:

''What are you going to think, I don't even get up to greet you, mademoiselle! But the doctor has forbidden it completely. And now I've gone such a long way with him I wouldn't want to lose him,'' she said, stroking her belly gently with her hand. ''But we didn't want this one, at the start.''

Her eyes grew moist again.

''Émile, yes, we wanted him, even though I was in bed six months before André came and we knew what I was in for. Antoine and I, we thought it was worth it all the same. But then, after Émile, we said, never again! Never again! But you see! I guess nature has its needs. . . .''

Émile was once more in the doorway, his little face craning to catch our conversation. His mother sent him back to mind the fire and sweep the kitchen.

And she took my hand again, smiling almost gaily through her tears.

''André's the one who'll be really pleased. He's doing the chores. We sent quite a few of the livestock to the farmer next door. An Icelander. A fine man he is! Thorgssen. But we still had to keep the milk-cow for ourselves. And the old horse in case Thorgssen was away. There's the chickens to feed, the cow to milk, the stable to clean. It's a lot for a child of eleven . . . not to mention meals.''

I took it on myself to ask her why she didn't accept help from Mrs. Badiou, who seemed quite ready to give it.

''Ah, yes!'' she answered. ''That's a good woman if there ever was one! But she has six children of her own, and the oldest isn't seven yet. One a year, never a miss.

99

And if her pregnancies are normal, her births are not. They go on forever. She was screaming for three days the last time. . . ."

Suddenly I couldn't stand it, and I wept with her over the lot of women.

"At least your husband will be back when . . ."

"Oh, if he only could! But his full winter's wages up there, that's our only salvation. Enough to finish our payments on the combine and get us out of debt. If we don't . . ."

The sound of feet stamping off snow made us stop talking. André came in, sent his cap flying to land on a nail in the wall, took off his jacket and stooped to unlace his high boots. His gestures, his attitude, his facial expression, were those of a man coming tired and a little deadened from his daily job. Émile, folding linen on the other side of the room, whispered to him, look . . . see who's there. . . .

André looked up and saw me sitting beside his mother. His face grew red with emotion. He came in, his hand stretched out, somewhat ceremoniously, but as soon as the greetings were over he leaned with solicitude toward his mother.

"No more pains? Are you all right?"

She stretched out her hand and, as I had so often wanted to do, smoothed back the lock of blond hair that fell over his eyes.

"Just fine," she said. "But we're going to keep your mademoiselle with us. Do you want to try an omelette?"

He agreed with joy and went off to the kitchen to put on a great apron with shoulder straps, and took his turn in issuing commands to little Émile:

"Now, then! Get some bark or kindling to get the fire up. A little speed, eh? No, get up on the chair and open the stovepipe draught and I'll bring some shavings."

Get up on the chair! Surely in all my life I had never heard this order repeated so often and so promptly obeyed.

Every time I looked out into the kitchen, there indeed was Émile standing on tiptoe on the chair to reach the Sunday crockery or fetch the best tablecloth from the high cupboard or close the stovepipe draught which was by now snoring too healthily.

André was busy too. His mother asked me to pull her bed over so that she could better observe the children at work, constantly giving them good advice:

"Beat your eggs till they're light, André."

I offered to help him.

She whispered:

"You mustn't. André likes to do it all by himself. He takes offence easily and anyway he has to get used to it."

At last I was invited to take my place at the table. I took a mouthful of omelette, and began to chew a tasteless substance with the texture of rubber. I succeeded, just the same, in swallowing the oversized serving André had given me. He watched me closely, and when I had downed the last forkful he said roughly to Émile:

"See? My omelette was good!"

Émile, making a face, shoved his plate away.

"I can't eat that. It's tough as an old boot."

I turned to the mother. We exchanged a furtive smile. André had brought her a small tray. She was eating, sitting up slightly in bed, with pillows behind her back.

For dessert they went and stood beside the bed, one on either side, each with a small dish, and fed her by the spoonful with viburnum jelly sent over by Thorgssen. They took turns in the process.

"One spoonful for André!"

"One for Émile!"

She was not hungry, but she gulped it down to please them.

I thought of the queen mother of the bees, fortified by her small servants to the best of their ability in her terrible task as funnel to the species.

When the meal had ended André set about washing the dishes from the morning and noon meals, helped by Émile who dried and, from his chair, put away the cups and plates.

I suggested that the mother sleep for a while, and I would rest as well, to prepare for an early start homeward, so as to arrive when it was still daylight.

She took my hand again.

"If you wanted to . . . If you'd just be kind enough to help André. I haven't been able to help him with his last arithmetic question. He's discouraged, he doesn't want to open his books these days, and I feel it's such a shame!"

I said that I'd help him, of course. He wiped the oilcloth tablecover with a damp rag, scratched with his nail at a stubborn spot, then went to bring all his school material, books, scribblers, ink bottle, until the big table was covered with it and the room looked like a school. Émile followed all our movements as if they were mysterious preparations for an unknown celebration.

I saw at once the difficulty that had caused André to stumble, and began explaining it to him. His face, grey with fatigue, suddenly grew heavy and lolled sideways, his eyes closing. He slept thus, sitting almost straight in his chair, for five or ten minutes. I didn't dare to move, but contemplated this defenceless face before me with a mixture of discomfiture and relief.

Nothing was left of him now but the fragile child. In his sleep, his head weighed to one side, he made me think of a flower bowing on its too-delicate stem. He woke as suddenly as he had gone to sleep, shook himself, apologized, attributed his "going-to-sleepiness" to the heat of the house, said that he was ready now to follow my explanations. And in fact I had the joy of seeing him understand at last. He was proud and happy.

"It's not so much for me, it's so I can help Émile later on when it's his turn."

"For you, too, my dear," his mother corrected him. "If only there was a way for you to get your year!"

I went over the problem again with André to make sure he had understood. I told him to keep the solution hidden somewhere and try to do the question a few times without looking it up. I also made a work plan for him, other arithmetic problems, a few rules of grammar, some guide marks that would help him work alone. He became tense as he tried to grasp the lesson, just as he had in school, his forehead reddening with effort and a kind of solemn joy. The time passed so quickly that I was surprised to hear the mother's soft voice saying from her room:

"Émile, my dear! I don't know how you can see a thing. Get up on a chair and take down the lamp. Bring it to me with a match. I'll brighten up the room for you."

I looked up from the scribblers and the open books. Above the edge of the combe, the plain was already pale and the sun had dropped below the horizon. A kind of mysterious happiness seemed to fill the darkened house. Émile was the first to yelp with joy:

"The lady won't be able to leave now. It's almost dark. She could be eaten by the wolves."

Less bubbling, but just as determined, André agreed:

"It's true, mademoiselle, you can't leave at this hour. Night would catch you on the way. We'd be too worried about you."

The mother backed them up:

"It's true, at this time it wouldn't be wise."

After a few seconds of hesitation I gave in to their objections. I was not that tempted, in any case, by the notion of venturing across the prairie with its lonely, tragic face at this time of day. The moment I nodded agreement a heartfelt activity took over the household, but all in an orderly way, with everything directed from the great iron bed.

"André, lift the trapdoor, go up to the big bedroom upstairs and get some linen sheets. The ones we brought

103

from France. You can hang them on some chair-backs, spread out, to warm them in front of the open fire. But right now, before you go upstairs, open the door of the other downstairs bedroom and let some heat in.''

They sent packing any fear of a chimney or stovepipe fire, stuffing the stove with lightwood which crackled merrily. Émile was asked to climb on a chair and regulate the draught by turning the handle once again. While the sheets, spread out from one chair-back to the next, grew warm they filled the room with a delicious smell.

What we ate for supper I don't remember. Unforgettable was the comforting, tender beauty of this interior, with its two lamps, one in the mother's room and one in the kitchen, their gleam reflected in the windowpanes which were invaded by the dark of night.

After supper the dishes and stable chores were done so quickly that I wondered if André had only half-milked the cow. Then Émile inquired:

"Are we going to have a party? A real party?"

As if relieved of the weight of his day's labour, André agreed indulgently. He went into the parlour, kept closed so that it need not be heated, brought out a phonograph with a horn speaker, which he set up on the table and cranked up. He put on a record. Out came something which remotely resembled an old Chevalier song. Mostly what I heard was a series of whistles, scratches and general caterwauling . . . then everything began to come apart. André hastened to give a few turns to the crank. The squeaks, the meeowing, the bleating, picked up again. The children were in seventh heaven.

Their three records played again and again. Émile came and knelt on the floor at my feet, planted his elbows on my knees and looked up at me with a supplicating air.

"Are you going to tell us a story?"

Sitting astride his chair like a man, his hands joined behind the chair-back, André nonetheless had an expression that agreed with Émile's request.

I asked them to come closer and then, O Lord, why did I start off, dead with fatigue as I was and wanting nothing better than to go to bed, with the long story of Aladdin and his wonderful lamp?

No doubt because of the miraculous effect brought about in this poor, isolated house by nothing more than the timid light of the lamp. But, as we all know, the story has no end.

I was falling asleep myself as I told it. I watched Émile as his eyes grew heavy and thought: There we go, he's dropping off, I'll be delivered at last. But he'd rub his eyes and hold them open forcibly until the sleepy spell passed and then spur me on without pity:

"Don't stop now! Your story's not finished!"

It came to an end at last. I went with the children to prepare their mother for the night and wish her rest. Then we all went to bed, I in the East Room, as they called it, Émile in a kind of little nook off the kitchen and André on a couch near his mother's room so that he could hear if she called.

In order to heat my room, André had built the fire up so high that I was far too warm even with the covers thrown back, and spent some time getting to sleep. But two hours later I awoke chilled to the bone.

The mother was calling softly, with the desire, one felt, not to really wake him up:

"André, the fire's out! It's getting cold! André!"

The call came again a little later. André seemed to hear nothing. I got up and went to the couch where he was sleeping. A white full moon, soft and peaceful, poured its light directly through the kitchen window. It fell on André's face, resting at last, with no cares, no anxiety, no weight of responsibility. His forehead was smooth, the lines of his mouth were pure. Suddenly I saw his half-open lips form the beginnings of a smile. What dream-thought had brought him relaxation at last?

In the light of the moon it was easy to find the makings

105

of a fire. As I waited to make sure it had caught properly, I went and sat beside the mother. Her eyes shone in the half-light. She had her rosary in her hands.

I asked her:

"When your time comes . . . what will you do?"

"That's easy," she reassured me. "André will run to Thorgssen, our good neighbour, and let him know. He'll hitch up and go for the doctor."

"And if the weather's bad?"

"Thorgssen will go anyway. He promised my husband. And anyway, you mustn't worry about me like this, mademoiselle. My pregnancies are hard but I give birth easily. You know, you can't have all the bad luck on your side."

I was going to go back to bed, but she took my hand with that touching gesture that I had seen several times already, as if to mark a deep need of her spirit, combined with confidence.

"If my husband comes back, as he's supposed to, about the end of April or the beginning of May, do you think it might be possible, in spite of everything, for André to pass his year? I'd give I don't know what for that."

In my heart I doubted it. I said only:

"I'll do my very best."

A pressure of her hand thanked me. I went back to bed after adjusting the draught of the stove yet again. This time I slept like a log. When I awoke it was broad daylight. The smell of freshly ground coffee and bread toasted over the flames wafted through the house.

Astonishingly, André succeeded in serving us an excellent breakfast. The butter especially had a very delicate taste, churned at home according to the mother's directions.

I said I had never tasted any with so fine a flavour since I used to visit my grandmother as a child. André blushed with pleasure.

No question of lingering this time. Under the high sun the plain was as it had been on the previous morning, a smooth, soft and shining sea. I would have to hurry to make the most of these luminous hours. I remembered the sudden, almost sinister coming of night that had surprised us yesterday in mid-afternoon. I said good-bye to the mother and the children who all at once grew serious when they saw me ready to leave.

I hurried away in the belated realization that while, by staying with the Pasquiers, I might have reassured them, I must have thrown my landlady in the village into a panic.

I came to the rim of the combe, passed it, climbed a little higher and reached a small knoll. There I stopped to look back. At the bottom of the funnel, I could still see the little lost farm.

Suddenly the back door opened. A silhouette appeared, the thin shoulders hunched forward. In one motion he sent the contents of a pail flying out on the snow and slipped the handle over his arm; then picked up a few sticks of firewood and some other object – perhaps a piece of clothing hung out to air – and went in, drawing the door shut behind him with a deft movement of his foot. Shortly after, a strong column of smoke rose out of the combe.

I went on my way, telling myself there's nothing to fear. The house is kept, well-kept.

Part 3

*I*n all my time as a teacher, had I ever been as frightened as I was of that child even before I saw him? I had barely arrived in all my innocence to take up my post in that isolated prairie village.

During the first days when everything seemed to be getting off to a good start between my pupils and myself, if, stopping for my mail at the general store, I happened to speak enthusiastically about the school, there would immediately be someone to dampen my ardour.

"Oh! Things are going well, are they? That's fine, that's fine! Just enjoy yourself. For it's going to be another story when you get Médéric."

They told me he'd held "the last teacher" at bay at the point of his jack-knife when she'd wanted to take the ruler to him. They said. . . . They said. . . . There wasn't one who didn't predict that there'd be war between us – war to the finish. And in fact it was to be war, but much more complex than the one they'd predicted, a mysterious war in which we confronted each other unarmed, each of us equally at a loss.

The first half of September had already passed. The heavy work was ending on almost all the farms. The harvested wheat was being driven off and piled up in the village's enormous silos from which, as I passed, I caught its acrid odour, loaded like no other smell with the slow, gentle ripenings of summer. My bigger pupils, who had been helping with the harvest, came back to school one after the other. All but Médéric! I waited for him, the more frightened as time passed and my imagination had the opportunity to construct an image of him that grew more detestable each day. Then one morning when I had quite forgotten him, there he was, taking me by surprise – just his style.

I was at the blackboard, writing down an arithmetic problem. Suddenly, behind me, total silence! I whirled around in alarm. The class was paying no attention to me. Big and small, they all had their eyes rivetted far across the prairie on a white spot that was rapidly approaching. The white spot became a horse with a black mane. Soon I could make out, crouching over the neck of his mount, a young rider who with wild gestures was urging his fiery steed, already flat-out, to greater efforts. On the back of his head he wore an immense cowboy hat. I was as captivated as the children by this spectacular arrival and knew at once that it must be Médéric.

Now he was at the entry of the schoolyard. Rather than taking the path, he pressed his horse at the barbed wire, jumped it, and continued at a gallop to the tall mast where the Union Jack was flying. In one leap he was on the ground by the flagpole, tying his horse which shook its head so furiously that the flag trembled as in a gust of wind.

After this fury of mounted speed he came along on foot without hurrying, ambling and swaggering to increase the suspense he knew he had created.

Finally, his big hat pushed down over his eyes, he

arrived in the doorway. There he stood, in high-heeled boots with Mexican designs, his legs apart, his hands deep in the pockets of his fringed pants, a studded belt around his hips. He took stock of us with an eye in which there was disdain and commiseration for the prisoners we were, and perhaps, beneath his swaggering, the awareness of his own solitude. Then, whistling as unconcernedly as if he had been walking down the street, he advanced down the centre aisle.

Like most country schoolrooms at the time, my class was furnished with double benches each attached to a long desk with an inkwell at either end, a groove for pencils and, below, two separate shelves.

Médéric arrived at the halfway point, where there was a desk occupied only by one of my smallest pupils. He flopped down beside him and with a nudge of his hip he sent the little one flying into the left aisle, then spread himself out to take up all the room. At the same time he threw me a glance in which there was not so much insolence as the desire to have a little fun here, if there was nothing better to do.

I helped up the little fellow, who was crying because he had landed on his bottom with all his things around him on the floor. I said, "Come along. You're better off sitting somewhere else than beside that big lout who's never learned how to behave."

My tongue was itching to go on in the same vein, but I controlled myself and went back to my lesson as if nothing had happened. But all I could think of was Médéric. I spied on him out of the corner of my eye, searching for the chink in his armour; and he may have been doing the same to me, for several times I saw him looking at me with annoyance and perhaps frustration at not having been able to get my goat. A moment later, however, when I imagined that I had perhaps caught his attention and was making an extra effort to hold it, he yawned in my face, his jaws wide apart, and stretched his long, thin legs out in the aisle. This put him in a position of being able to trip anyone who walked that way. He barely condescended to pull them back a little when I went past.

And I let him continue; what could I do? I was eighteen and he was going on fourteen. He was easily a head taller than I and no doubt at least that far ahead of me in other aspects of life.

So it was that from the very start, without intention on my part, what served me best against Médéric was my own helplessness. Not knowing how to handle a boy of that age, daring nothing, saying nothing, but putting on a bold front with my distant, inaccessible air, I succeeded in irritating him beyond measure. Bored, unable to make me lose patience, he began to tear up the pages of his scribbler, roll them into balls, dip them in glue and then, using his ruler as a catapult, shoot them to the ceiling where they stuck. Having started this game, which didn't amuse him for long because I paid no attention, he felt obliged to keep it up, though it bored him more and more. And so the day went by. At four o'clock, as the class was about to leave, I called him back, pronouncing his name for the first time:

"Médéric Eymard!"

He whirled around in a posture of self-defence, his eye sharp, his fists closed.

"I just wanted to talk to you. Unless you're scared!"

He looked around, searching for complicity among the others, expecting them to laugh at the simple-minded notion that he might be afraid of me. Had he lost his lead already? Not many caught his eye. The rows drained off, leaving him alone in the middle of the classroom like a chunk of driftwood on the beach. He went back to his seat, still swaggering. Soon, in the ensuing silence, he began to bite his fingernails.

At my desk, I was searching for composure. I tidied papers. I looked into exercise books. I pretended to be absorbed in my work. In fact, I was waiting for my heart to settle down. At last I dared to look up at him, and it seemed to me that he was just as troubled. The notion of speaking to him as teacher to pupil across all that distance was ridiculous. I rose, walked to his desk and, a little fearfully, wrapping my skirt around me, sat down at the opposite end of his bench. He shifted slightly to give me more room. We remained there, staring straight ahead in silence, for I don't know how long. With a toss of my head I threw back my hair, of which a few strands always hung over my eyes. I risked a glance at Médéric. Then I realized that he was, after all, still a child, with a fragile neck and a tall but delicate body. His eyes, which were looking anywhere but at me, struck me particularly. They were of a colour between blue and violet such as I had never seen in all my life and never have since. They made me think of the rare shades that sometimes tinge a summer sky after sunset.

Under his long, thick lashes they now seemed embarrassed, abashed and troubled. I remembered my landlady's advice: "Don't let yourself be taken in by Médéric's angel eyes. It's for sending others to perdition he's got eyes like that." Sitting near him, silent, I was intimidating him severely without either of us understanding how it had come about. That silence which I maintained at my end of the bench was my advantage over him, though I didn't know it.

At last I spoke, as if I were talking to myself:

"Suppose the school inspector came around, or the priest – they say he doesn't really like a joke – or just somebody from the school board, and they asked me, 'Where did that funny decoration on the ceiling come from?' What could I answer but this: 'From my biggest pupil, can you imagine that? And I have no authority over him because he's a good half a foot taller than I am. . . . ' "

I paused.

" '. . . and he's the only one big enough to unstick all that, if he'd take the trouble.' "

Without taking his eyes off the point he was staring at, far ahead of him, Médéric acknowledged the message with a shrug and a look of irritation at having to admit that I was right.

Abruptly he got up from his desk and went to fetch the stepladder from the back of the room. He climbed up and with the broom he toiled at undoing his day's work. From below I urged him on:

"Over here! Over there again!"

When he came down, red with the effort, he seemed less offended than astonished that I had been able to turn him into a charwoman. He stared at me with a mixture of defiance and embarrassment. But, above all, he was in a hurry to leave; and suddenly, without any greeting, he was outside. He leapt on his horse, pushed his big hat back on his neck, took off at high speed, exciting the animal with his voice, and soon was nothing more than a speck of white and dark on the immensity of the naked plain. His ride, a spectacle this time intended for me alone, seemed now to be the admission of a solitude that is never so profound as in the very last days of childhood.

I was wrong, however, if I thought Médéric was tamed. True, he never again put my authority in peril before the others. He pretended to conform to the rules of the game. He even consented to separate himself from his cowboy hat during school hours. As he took it off one morning he went so far as to wave it in such a sweeping salute that it couldn't be taken for a courtesy. But apart from those moments when he was one of us, at least for purposes of making fun of the school, he was always elusive. I deployed an incredible inventiveness

116

to get his attention. At times, just for a moment, attracted in spite of himself, he would look at me as if he were going to let himself be caught, but suddenly he was gone again. He was off in some reverie, disdainful of us all. That grieved me, though I often secretly wished that this undisciplined wretch would simply go away. My class had been working so well before he came. Why, I wondered, did I have to inherit this phenomenon? Two or three times I tried to pay no attention, to leave him, if that was what he wanted, to his ignorance, his idleness; but I couldn't keep it up, and was possessed again by the frenzied desire to make him progress. That was the kind of fever I had then – imperious as love, for it was a kind of love – the passionate need I have felt all my life to try and bring out the best in everyone.

I went back to Médéric and used every trick I knew to capture this restless mind. It happened a few times that I awoke a glimmer of passing interest, but he fled me again. Sometimes as I looked at him, so near and yet so ready to escape, I had the impression of an innocent animal that will perhaps end up allowing itself to be trapped; and even as I was wishing for its capture I felt a certain regret on its behalf. In the freedom of his dreams Médéric must have wandered very far, because when I lost my patience and called him back rather sharply he took some time to return; and on each occasion the shock of finding himself behind a desk made him give a little shudder, as if trying to shake off a fetter.

I came to feel some hesitation about bringing him back from his imaginary travels. Not that they were always happy trips! From a darkening of his eyes I guessed that they occasionally took him back to certain painful memories. But they also carried him to that impregnable refuge that children create for themselves at their most vulnerable age. It was from these travels that I had scruples about awakening him. I had barely recovered from those reveries myself, had just passed beyond my adolescent dreams, and was so little resigned to my adult life that sometimes, when I saw my small pupils appear in the early morning on the prairie as fresh as the dawning of the world, I wanted to run toward them and place myself forever on their side instead of waiting for them in the snare of school.

"Come, Médéric, come back!"

As I had adopted a way of calling him more gently, he didn't fail to come back for a moment and sometimes even gave a smile as he recognized me.

I had not given him a desk companion, realizing that he wouldn't have put up with anyone. Who could it have been, in any case? Backward as he was for his age, I would have had to choose someone younger than he, which would have humiliated him and made him feel his isolation more. So the right side of his desk was free, and without particularly noticing, I had got into the habit of sitting beside him when I had a problem to explain to him alone. Unconsciously I must have noticed that when I stood beside this lanky adolescent I seemed slight and small, and imagined that I lost stature and authority in his eyes. On the other hand, if I had him come to me at my desk it was he, thin and awkward, leaning over to follow the lesson, who lost in prestige. To avoid these annoyances, I began to go and sit at the other end of his bench when the passion possessed me to get a lesson into his head. Then it became a natural thing to do, and I went there often, but taking care to leave between us as much space as possible. One day, through carelessness, our knees touched and he withdrew his with the alacrity of a skittish animal. For the rest, he seemed to accept as a normal thing that I should sit beside him, for I did the same with many other children, though they were smaller than Médéric. By persisting in talking to him eye to eye I hoped to gain some ground and awaken him to a taste for learning.

If I had been more experienced I might have noticed that in this process he gained as much as I did, and often had the upper hand.

One day, with the grammar book open between us, I was making a supreme effort to teach him the rule of agreement of participles, and I saw from his expression that he wasn't listening. His gaze wandered over the fields outside and for a moment revealed such a desire to be out there that I, who had never seen a prisoner, imagined that this must be how they would gaze out at the wide horizon. At that very moment Gaspard, the white stallion with the black mane tied to the flagpole, raised his fine head and turned it toward the school. I had often asked Médéric to tie him somewhere else, remarking that the school inspector, who was to visit us any day, would surely have something to say about what might seem like an affront to the flag of His Britannic Majesty. Médéric had made a face, as if to say that as far as he was concerned it was an honour for His Britannic Majesty to have his emblem associated with such a noble beast. Just the same, he had more or less undertaken to do as I asked, but the little flagpole mound was the only place from which Gaspard, when he was very bored, could look into the classroom. At such times he gave a strange, soft, supplicating whinny that made us all lose track of the lesson. I knew that Médéric would never deprive Gaspard of the consolation of seeing the children through the window. I didn't push him, hoping that the inspector's visit wouldn't come before the snows. ". . . for then," Médéric had told me, "if by chance I'm still in school I'll have to find a warm stable for Gaspard some place nearby."

Well, there I was that day – I remember it very well – talking about French "participles that agree if . . . and, on the other hand, don't agree in the case of . . ." when Gaspard turned toward us his slim, handsome head. A second later in the afternoon silence came his vibrant cry of reproach.

119

It wasn't Gaspard's usual whinny. It was as if he wanted to let us know how mad it was to spend your life tied up, he to his pole and we, pupils and teacher, to our desks. The complaint must have touched us all, for we looked up together and stared, escaping through the window in a silent swarm. The day was so beautiful it took your breath away, and we'd barely found the time to notice. Far away, near the tense, bright-blue horizon, a low line of bushes, glowing in autumn colours, seemed to be on fire. The illusion of the flaming bush was so strong that the air above seemed to tremble, as if over coals.

With great difficulty I came back from the contemplation of a magnificent moment that devoured itself and yet remained the same. And I immediately attacked my dreamer.

"Médéric, where are you?"

Without conceding a glance, he did give me the smile of one who is about his secret business but doesn't wish to be rude to the intruder.

"I'll bet," I said, "that you're galloping on Gaspard over to that little thicket, the one that's on fire."

This time he looked at me. His eyes were veiled with his dream. Just a trace of it remained – that thin film, slightly misted over, that is there just before the dream dissolves, a fragile frontier between this side of things and that other side.

"No," he said, as if against his will, perhaps unaware that he was beginning to open up to me, "today, if there wasn't any school, I'd be up in the Babcock hills."

I myself had an obsessive picture of those little hills which the train had passed through as I came to take up my job in the village, and almost every day I told myself I must go back and visit them.

"From the train," Médéric said scornfully, "you don't see a thing. You've got to go on horseback, or walking." And he added, more softly, ". . . alone."

120

"Oh, I can see how you'd like those wild places," I couldn't help taunting him. "That's not hard to imagine. But what is there for Gaspard away up there?"

"Some special grass," said Médéric, having his turn to be patient at my ignorance, "and the sharp air, but especially he likes to look far around."

"But I thought horses were short-sighted."

"That may be," Médéric conceded, "but you put a horse out to pasture where there's a little high place with a view, and that's where you'll find him a few hours later, as high as he can get, and happy."

"That's true enough," I said, astonished at the precision of his observation, and he was as pleased as if I had paid him a compliment. But why did I have to spoil it all by adding:

"If you concentrated on your class work the way you do on nature you'd be a real ace."

He gave me to understand that this concerned him hardly at all. But without showing any ill-humour. On the contrary, he was almost friendly, and I soon understood why. He wanted to exploit my moment of weakness to extort something from me.

"Mamzelle, would you let me go and water Gaspard? I'll be quick."

It wasn't long since recess, and he'd taken the horse then to the trough at the back of the schoolyard. So it wasn't water he wanted to give Gaspard. I looked at him and thought: Really, he's just like his horse, obeying nothing but affection; and perhaps one day he too will belong heart and soul to his master, if he finds one to tame him.

"All right," I said grudgingly. "Run out and tell Gaspard to be patient, the day's almost finished. But hurry up, you'll get me in trouble with the village with your fun and fancies."

"Oh, the village!" he said with a kind of happy commiseration, and flew off to murmur a few words of encouragement to Gaspard, I suppose, for I didn't see him untie the horse, he just held him close as if he were talking in his ear; and the horse, lowering his head, tossed it quickly a few times, as if in assent: Very well, I'll try to hang on, but you hurry up and get through with school.

When he came back, happy to have come to a deal with Gaspard and perhaps to have breathed the fresh air whose tang you could smell on his clothes, I was irritated at seeing him happier outside the school than in, and I made the inopportune remark:

"Really, Médéric Eymard, if you hate school as much as you seem to, I don't know why you come at all."

The violet of his eyes turned to night. I saw for the first time with my own eyes the angry boy, enraged, ready to break and spoil, the boy whom everyone had described to me when I arrived in the village. He controlled himself, however, as if he thought I wasn't really worth lashing into. He answered brusquely:

"It's because of my father. He makes me come. If it wasn't for that, you can be sure I wouldn't stay a day longer in your damned school. He's got the law on his side. He's had the police after me twice, last spring when I tried to get a job on a farm, and another time when I sneaked off with my haversack to the Babcock hills."

"Oh, Médéric, but how could I know that?"

To show my regret, I found nothing better than placing my hand on his, which was resting on the desk. Mine covered no more than half of it. He noticed the fact, measuring our hands with an absent look, and in spite of his inner turmoil must have been touched by it, for he observed, in an odd, gruff but engaging way: "Hey, you've got small hands, mamzelle!" and pulled his own away to hide it under the desk. A shade of suffering remained in his eyes and I undertook to banish it.

"Have you tried getting away in the hills this year?"

"Just for two days. My dad's on the lookout now. They found me almost right away, brought me back like a thief. . . ."

He was shaking silently with a pent-up resentment. He lifted his head defiantly and said:

"I'll soon be fourteen. My dad can't force me to go to school anymore. I'll be free."

The word was like a trumpet sounding and reminded me that not so long ago I too had thought that freedom was what I wanted most of all.

"What will you do with . . . your freedom?"

"I'll . . . I'll . . ."

"Even your Gaspard that you're so fond of isn't free. Look, he lives at the end of a rope."

"That's because he has to wait for me. But the day I get free I'll set him free too."

"And what will he do, the poor thing? He'll come galloping back to you and if he can't find you he'll die of grief."

Médéric looked down, astonished, saddened.

"I suppose you're right. So being free . . ." and he trembled on the verge of a premonition that perhaps nothing in life is quite up to what you think it is at thirteen.

"There may be other things, better . . . "

"Like what?"

"Oh, I don't know. Work, for some people. Duty. For others it may be love. Or an attachment of some kind."

"Thank you, no. Not for me! For me it'll always be freedom."

I left him with his notions. But it seemed to me that from that day on he was a little shaken and began to listen with some concentration, even making a real effort to keep up with the class.

At the very time when he was struggling against his penchant for dreaming, it was I, at the end of my rope, who started losing my grip. The long, low fire that went on burning at the sky's edge had put me in a state of revolt. Young as I was, I saw myself shut up for life in my work as a teacher. I lost sight of the exciting side of it and thought only of its implacable routine. To tell the truth, I didn't know what kind of state I was in. One day I'd be concerned as ever about my pupils' progress, the next I would be overtaken by melancholy. The last radiant days of fall were ending, reproaching me with bypassing without enjoyment what is perhaps the most priceless thing in the world. When Gaspard issued his call to freedom, it was I who looked up and out to the high, detached sky. I wondered: What is really worth giving your talent to, and your life?

One day as I passed Médéric's desk I leaned over to glance at his composition, but instead of talking about it I heard myself ask:

"Those hills of yours, they're really only hillocks, aren't they?"

He snatched up his pencil and in strong, lively strokes, with surprising talent, he sketched in a squat little mountain, put a tree here and there, a few blocks of fallen rock, bushes on the slopes, and with such spare means managed to create the atmosphere of a place totally cut off from the world, appealing in its profound secrecy.

Seated at the end of his bench, I enjoyed seeing this wild spot come to life.

"In the middle," said Médéric, tracing its course, "there's a creek. I followed it one day, right to where it starts. Four hours' walking! It's not easy to find, it's hidden under a fallen tree. The water's like ice. An English guy had a cabin up there a few years back, and he must have seeded the stream with trout. There's still trout there, and do you know, mamzelle, the funniest thing . . ."

From the moment he started talking about the hills he appeared like a child set free, at ease, breathing deeply. On the point of going on with his confidences he hesitated a

124

second, stared into my eyes to make sure I was interested and, reassured, went on in the excitement of sharing with me what was so important to him.

"What then, Médéric?"

"Well, the trout go right to the source sometimes, and when they're up there in that icy water they let you take them in your hand, you can hold them and touch them. What do you think of that?"

"Maybe it's the cold of the water," I said, guessing, "making them numb."

"You can hold them and stroke them," he said again, dreaming, and his languid, violet eyes showed love at its height of delicacy. And I discovered once more, and with the same deep surprise, that the first burgeoning of love, in adolescence, is for the small, free creatures of the earth and its waters. I saw gliding over his face the joyous trembling he had felt at holding in his hands, tame and consenting, the most timorous fish in the world; and I thought it would soon be his turn to be tamed, vulnerable as I now discovered him to be, if I could muster the skill to do it.

Another time he told me how he had found in the wildest part of the hills a heap of dry bones, so old and worn by time that you couldn't tell what animals they belonged to. Was this a cemetery where they had gone by themselves to die, as the story had it? Or was it the site of a cruel ambush in which they had been caught by men of other times?

"More likely that, I would think."

He seemed satisfied by my reply, and from then on inclined to believe that there were things to be learned from me, even in areas that seemed unlikely.

He even told me about his most astonishing discovery: up there, right at the summit of the hill, imprinted in the stone. "Is there an explanation for that, mamzelle? The shape of a fish!"

"A fossil! Yes, it's possible. The Sea of Agassiz covered

almost all the interior of our continent many, many years ago. It's to be expected that the water, when it drew back, left traces of marine life or shellfish, even on the hilltops.''

I was doing my scientist act, and he, dazzled, seemed ready to credit almost anything I might say. I took advantage of the moment and said:

"If you'd read a little, Médéric, instead of relying on your trotters to explore, you'd see that books are full of wonders too.''

I sent him to get one of the volumes of the encyclopedia that I had managed to squeeze out of our poor board of trustees for the school. I told him to look under the heading Agassiz. Together we read the long paragraph on the subject. Afterwards, I saw the same eyes overflowing with dreams that I had seen as he spoke of the trout that let themselves be touched in the icy water.

"That says exactly what I saw!'' he cried in the happy surprise of finding his discovery confirmed by the big, impressive book.

I can say that I knew the very moment when the love of books was awakened in Médéric. But the curious thing was that no sooner had he discovered the pleasure of finding in written form the movement, the surprises, the enigmas of life, than I myself dreamed only of going back beyond books to what had given birth to them and was not exhausted by them.

"Your hills," I asked him another day, "are they inhabited?"

"Not a soul!'' he said triumphantly. "We're always alone, Gaspard and I.''

Going from one feeling to another, I was on the point of reproaching him with a taste for solitude that I found exaggerated at his age, but I recalled in time that I had just emerged from a period during which I had practically lived with my back turned to other people. I suppose that before

126

we experience love we are gripped by a foreboding that it will be the source of the essential suffering in our lives, and we try our best to hide from it, huddled in frail shelters or, like Médéric, taking refuge in the whole, innocent earth.

He now shared his fierce joys openly and there was scarcely a day that passed without his coming with some rare grass or a bird's nest hard to find in those parts. One day he brought, warm beneath his jacket, a live bird that he was going to set free as soon as I had had a look, because we had come across its picture in a coloured bird book and – "you said, mamzelle, that you'd like to see one."

Although I had crossed the border of the kingdom where only yesterday I, like Médéric now, had been at home, I longed to return there with him as guide, imagining that it would be possible in his footsteps to regain access to the lost frontier.

One day when I kept him in after the others to go over a problem, and we were seated side by side, alone in the classroom that was still bright with the reddish light of the distant thicket, I asked him point-blank, without stopping to think what mad slope I was starting down: "Tell me, Médéric, are those hills of yours very far away?"

"Why, no! If you take my shortcut it's no more than nine miles."

A little later, slowly, he began to understand why I had asked the question.

"Would you like to go there?"

It was too late to protest. He had seen through me, and his expression let me know that he felt at last he had the upper hand.

"With a good horse it's easy. We'd be there in three hours, starting from the village, mamzelle."

His tone was affectionate, pleading, and his eyes as well, their violet turned soft.

"So you can go there and back in a day?"

"And we'd still have lots of time, mamzelle!"

Hastily, to close the door on the idea, I said:

"But I don't have a horse."

"I've got a little mare, she's gentle as can be," he said. "She won't shake you up at all, mamzelle. If you like I'll come and get you early next Saturday, can I?"

"Not so fast, not so fast!"

"But it's almost the end of fall."

"November could still be nice."

"But . . ."

I was reflecting, not on the imprudence I was almost consenting to, but, strangely enough, through the confusion of my thoughts, on the leverage I could acquire from the passionate wish I had awakened in Médéric to show me his hills. I stared into his eyes. There was nothing there but an adolescent exultation at the notion of sharing, with someone he felt was worthy of it, his love of a world which until then he had explored so completely alone that he needed my confirmation of its infinite splendour. Médéric was suddenly taken by a burning need to be reassured by me as to the beauty of his wild retreat.

"Shall we make a pact, you and I?"

In his eyes I glimpsed a shade of that haughty contempt for the adult world that the child never feels so strongly as just before he enters it.

"You mean a deal?"

"If you like, but it's a fair one. You learn all this," and I indicated a good slice of the grammar book, "and as soon as you know your conjugations, maybe in two weeks, I'll go with you to the Babcock hills."

How did he do it? I still don't know. In the end-of-the-month test, did he manage to copy from a neighbour? Hardly: I was keeping too close an eye on him. Had he been snooping in my desk to see the test paper, so as to prepare himself for the questions? I doubt it. All I really knew is that his marks this time were a healthy average, whereas before he had been far behind the others. I gave him his report and when he saw the marks he gave a whistle of mocking admiration as if he were congratulating himself ironically. I fancied I caught a trace of faintly impertinent triumph. But a second later he seemed merely happy at having won his bet.

Early the next Saturday, after a night of light frost that had purified the air and left a sting in it, he was at my door, riding Gaspard and leading Flora, a gentle little mare that I loved at once, in her simple robe of bay relieved by a stripe of white that went from her forelock to her nostrils and gave her thin head a pensive air.

For more than two hours we had been riding silently uphill, Médéric in the lead. Among the stacked blocks of stone held in the strangest equilibrium, we did not see, until the very last moment, any hint of the narrow pass we were to climb toward country still wilder and more intractable.

At times Médéric would stop, sniffing the air, which seemed to guide him as much as sight itself; and then, with astonishing flair, he spotted the gap where I had seen nothing but tangled brush. Despite its lateness in the season, the day promised to be one of brilliant sunshine, a rare thing in our countryside where snow and storms come early. I mentioned this to Médéric, who smiled knowingly, as if he had expected nothing else. From then on we barely spoke, concentrating on the hard ascent. Occasionally, Médéric would look back and his face, under the wide-brimmed hat, would light up briefly for my benefit, to encourage me along and, no doubt, to promise a reward for all our efforts.

We were off again, attacking yet another steep hillside. Showers of pebbles kicked off by our horses' hooves rolled down the slopes. Sometimes a single stone would reach the bottom long after the others, and its solitary fall, amid that profound and meditative silence, would echo unforgettably.

Then came another narrow corrie and we were enclosed again in an oppressive silence. In the shadow of the dull-grey rocks we could hardly glimpse the sun or any hint of the radiant day ahead, except for stray darts of light from time to time. This closed-in landscape never opening out, climbing in an ever-tightening spiral, depressed me. My school, the village, my life down below, seemed to have been friendly but long forsaken. Even Médéric's form from the back seemed unfamiliar. I suddenly remembered that it was with a boy about whom I really knew very little that I was venturing into this hostile, uninhabited country. A twinge of fear touched my heart. Then Médéric turned around, all smiles beneath his gigantic hat, to point triumphantly ahead toward the goal we had been pursuing for the last few hours.

The blocks of stone, with their sinister forms, drew back gradually. A large slice of sky pushed through between rocky peaks. And the plain was ours again, even more visible because we had lost it for several hours, the great stretch of land motionless but nonetheless endowed with an irresistible, sweeping movement.

How can I ever forget that sight? Even today when that memory returns, my soul swells with contentment and happiness. What is it about the view from a certain height that fills us with such elation? Is it the fact of having struggled to come so high? I still don't know. What I believe to be certain is that I had never seen the prairie so awesome in all its breadth, its fullness, its noble sadness, its transfigured beauty, as I did that morning from the saddle with Médéric, our two horses standing side by side.

Near the azure sky, freshly ploughed earth matched in

its glossy black the dark bird circling above. On higher ground, where the night's hoar-frost still clung to the clods of earth, they together composed the most delicate of charcoal sketches. Far in the distance we could see a tiny square of tender green, no doubt a patch of young fall wheat, like a captive springtime in its small corral. Yet it was not by any one of its aspects, even the most rare, that the prairie caught one's heart, but, on the contrary, because at last they all disappeared, were swallowed by it. Although at the start one saw this or that, and especially the patch of springtime in its enclosure, soon one was conscious only of the immutable. Waves disappear in the sea, trees in the forest, and in a like way after a time almost every hint of human life, almost every detail, vanishes in the infinite surface on the plain. Saying nothing in particular, perhaps it is thus that it finally says so much.

I looked at Médéric. From under his hat, now pulled over his eyes, he was spying on me with intense curiosity, watching me contemplate the plain, waiting for the first sign of the happiness he had hoped to provide me in this strange, high place. Now that he saw me beaming, he beamed as well. Was it a pure gift on his part? Or did he feel the need, as is often the case in young lives, to share what he possessed in order to know it perfectly? We looked at each other with eyes that must have been filled with the same splash of joy. Then softly we began to laugh. It was a light, gentle laughter, a lazy laughter. Why were we laughing? Perhaps at finding ourselves so happy together, joining in the rare and marvellous understanding between two people that makes words or gestures unnecessary.

Then we grew silent again, and serious. Each attentive to the landscape that united us. Like all great, free spaces, what it inspired in us must have been that dream-like but unshakeable confidence in life and what we will become, the face that will be ours in time. It occurs to me now that moments of sheer confidence I have had in my life were all connected with this same happy vagueness that we were

131

lucky enough to feel that day, Médéric and I, on the narrow plateau carved into a lookout on the hills' crest. I imagine that just as we saw far out in the distance, we ourselves could have been seen by those below in their farmhouses flat on the plain, had they raised their eyes to the two silhouettes on the escarpment's edge.

How long did we stay there, almost without moving, still in our saddles so as to see a shade farther and perhaps glimpse the future unfolding before our eyes? Finally Médéric, partly recovered from the reverie that had overtaken us, suggested playfully:

"How would you like, mamzelle, to go and see if the trout are waiting for us?"

I agreed enthusiastically and wheeled Flora around to follow him. He was already taking off and shouting not to look down, for I had said I was a little dizzy.

In the narrow valley where he brought me, after turns, half-turns and hairpin turns, I saw a trickle of clear water tumbling from beneath a great tree that death had laid down in the posture of a man drinking from the stream.

Médéric slid his hand beneath the slippery trunk. He felt in the water, this way, that way. A ray of sunlight, fighting through to us, turned our hands and faces pink. At the same moment Médéric's face lit up with the inner light of joy and elation. Before, on the crest of the plain, I had seen him in the power of a grave, peaceful joy, rare at his age. Here he was prey to all that can be feverish and agitating in the joy of childhood.

"They're here, mamzelle! One just slid past my hand. Hey, there he is again! He's letting me catch him. He's in my hand, mamzelle!"

For fear of scaring the fish, he was shouting in a whisper, or whispering a shout – I don't know how to describe it – but he was in the grip of an exuberance that he could scarcely control.

"Try it, mamzelle, try it!" he begged me eagerly.

With a feeling of repugnance, I put my hand into the icy water. I fancied I felt a touch at my fingertips, but thought it must be weeds at the water's bed. Then suddenly into my half-open hand slipped a little creature, smooth, soft, undulating. It did not try to escape when I closed my hand gently around it. A prisoner, it seemed to take pleasure in turning and wriggling between my fingers. I was just as ecstatic as Médéric.

"I wouldn't have believed you," I said, "if I hadn't done it myself."

"It's hard to believe," he admitted.

Now he was on his knees in the grass at the spring's edge, his hands in the water. The sparkle in his eyes showed his pleasure at feeling a wild thing tame at his fingertips. On opposite sides of the spring, face to face, we described our experiences which were so identical that the same happy smile came to our lips.

"Have you got one, mamzelle?"

"Yes, I think so . . ."

"Is he staying? Does he let you touch him?"

"Yes, yes, he does!"

"Let him go a little . . . see if he comes back. . . . Did he come back?"

"He came back . . . but is it the same one?"

He sat up on his heels in the rough, tangled grass, brushed at his hat with an arm and said:

"Mamzelle, you've read a lot, you've learned a lot of things. How do you explain that the trout here aren't afraid of us?"

"You could explain that better than I can," I said. "You know more about nature's secrets than I do."

He smiled in embarrassment and answered a little gruffly:

"Oh, come on, mamzelle, you're kidding!"

Our hands went back in the water. The trout came again

133

to play in them with their inexplicable abandon.

"It's a mystery," said Médéric, his voice and his eyes expressing a deep reverence, though there was in his gaze a slow dawning of a distant sadness that threatened the privilege of being in the midst of so many joys. He murmured: "There's mystery everywhere, don't you think?"

I nodded. I thought it might be the spawning season that made the trout so vulnerable. Or the extreme cold of the water. Later I was to search for all sorts of rational explanations for the phenomenon at the spring. But nothing can change the fact that Médéric and I knew the most innocent of joys when we thought these timid creatures were tamed within our hands and taking pleasure in our company.

"It would be easy to catch some for our lunch," I said, joking.

"Oh, mamzelle, that would be a crime!"

"Why?"

"Well, because . . . here . . . they're . . . trus . . . ting."

When he used words with an emotional meaning he stuttered slightly, really only hesitating but almost painfully, as if he were fearful of a new weapon he was not yet sure he could handle.

"But we're going to catch some down there and roast them in the pan, as you promised. Where's the difference?"

He looked at me, surprised:

"Why, the ones down there aren't trusting us. They'll have their chance to escape. It's not the same thing."

"You're quite right. It's not the same thing."

We lingered, first at the strange pile of whitened bones, then to rest and eat a little, farther still to examine the fossils in a rock wall, and the day went by without our knowing it.

It was only on the way back, in the dusk that was already

nearly dark, the horses' hooves ringing on the deserted main street but no doubt spied on from every window, that I realized I had exposed Médéric and myself to the malevolence of the village. I fancied I could feel their disapproving gaze follow us from house to house, where they had delayed lighting lamps to better make us out in the night-blue air; for behind us, as we passed, the windows lit up one by one. The pure joy that had filled the day from end to end was sullied, a drop of gall spreading in clear water.

They can go to the devil! I thought.

I dismounted, patted my horse in thanks and staggered to the door, hurting all over, and saw Médéric leading Flora slowly away, accommodating his pace to that of the exhausted young animal. Then, in that vague light in which they disappeared, less precise than night itself, I had the impression that I would never again see the two creatures walking side by side and the child that guided them, encouraging them with little words of kindness that slowly melted into the half-dark.

Apart from the encyclopedia, I have to admit that books were not able to hold Médéric's attention very long. But he loved those thick volumes, heavy to handle and full of illustrations and information on the subjects that fascinated him, to the exclusion of almost every other source of learning. He burrowed in it continually, searching for corroboration of what he had discovered by himself in nature or merely imagined. Sometimes he was so pleased at finding his knowledge confirmed by science that he would come up to me, the great book open in his hands, and show me the passage:

"See, mamzelle? The bird I told you about, it really was

a great horned owl.''

At times I would get in the spirit of his games, as happy as he was to connect book learning with something I had been intrigued by, or some question I had been asked during the day. But I forced myself to be strict, perhaps because I knew that I could now do so without being threatened by a beating, but also because I wanted to draw back a little from what might have been undue familiarity.

Then, seeing his eyes and their candour when he brought me some new treasure from the fields or woods, I would lose my resolve, disarmed by the naïve side of him.

One day I said to my landlady:

"That Médéric may be tall as a man but he's such a child, really, you wouldn't believe it."

"Do you believe it?" she asked with a curiously incisive tone, giving me a piercing look.

· Not long after that, one fine morning Médéric came with news that created a sensation in the school and, for that matter, all through the village.

"My father went to town and bought me the whole encyclopedia," he told me. "Twelve volumes! We're going to spend some good evenings at home together now."

I was speechless.

No one could doubt that Médéric's father had money enough to buy the expensive collection. The surprise came from the fact that he was considered ignorant, uncouth and gross in his ways. Yet from that day on, Médéric spoke of his father without the slightest hostility but rather with some deference.

"He likes to read about telling the future," Médéric told me, "predictions, the stars, signs in the sky and Nostradamus, you know? And the schisms in the Church. And the divided popes . . . and the Borgias. . . ."

I couldn't help smiling, for the headings he mentioned told so much about his home and, in a way, about Médéric himself.

Yet I was vaguely concerned. His too-sudden complicity with his father, the latter's new generosity to Médéric, were somehow disquieting. I asked my landlady what sort of man Rodrigue Eymard really was. She told me a surprising story. In his youth he had been handsome, seductive, already rich. He had courted and eloped with a half-Indian girl. The idyll hadn't lasted long. Shortly after Médéric was born the young woman disappeared. Some said it was Rodrigue who had showed her the door, others that she left at night, on horseback, to rejoin the tribe she came from, which protected her against her husband's efforts to take her back. Several times she had tried to see the child but with no success, for the courts had given custody to the father. Whatever the facts, Rodrigue Eymard had from that time begun to go to seed, drank too much, gave signs of mental disturbance, occasionally struggling to regain control of himself but always sliding back into a life of excess. How much was true in all these rumours? My landlady herself admitted they must contain some exaggerations. What was certain, she told me, was that Médéric lived alone with his father in an immense house called "The Castle" – though its housekeeping was done in a desultory way by a woman from the neighbourhood who did some cooking and perhaps performed other services for the master.

This put Médéric's life in a totally unexpected light. And lo and behold, he came to me shortly after with a ceremonious invitation from his father to have dinner with them the following Sunday.

What should I say? A foreboding of unpleasantness to come left me paralyzed.

"Do you really want me to come, you yourself, Médéric?"

In reply, he seemed to be reciting something his father had said, and the growing influence of Rodrigue surprised me more and more, and frankly, frightened me. I recalled

137

that he recently stressed how much money they had, something I had never noticed before and not typical of his nature.

"We're the only family you haven't honoured with a visit," he said reproachfully. "Anybody'd think the Eymards' is the only place you wouldn't set foot in. My father says if you refuse it's an insult."

"You know very well," I told him, "that I haven't been in any house where there are only men."

If I'd hoped to get out of it that way, I hadn't reckoned with Médéric, who had his answer all ready:

"There'll be a woman. The neighbour that comes to work for my father. And he says you can be sure she'll give you a dinner fit for a king."

I tried to escape by another route. The Eymard farm was more than three miles from the village. Médéric lived farther from the school than any of my pupils, and in winter the road out his way was exposed to strong winds that often blew drifts as high as the rig.

"You can never tell in wintertime if you're even going to get to your place."

"I'll come and get you . . . mamzelle."

I asked my landlady's advice about Médéric's invitation.

"Don't you go there!" she cried. "Since his wife left him Rodrigue Eymard is like a madman. For the love of heaven, don't go into that house."

But Médéric was insistent:

"My father says if the weather gets bad you don't have to worry. He'd let me have the berline to come and get you."

He seemed so delighted at this prospect that I asked him:

"Does the berline mean so much to you?"

"Mamzelle," he said, "I've been trying to get to drive it for two years, and for once when he'll let me . . ."

That's how I gave in, more or less against my will, for I felt obliged to put myself on Médéric's side in the whole

138

business, which everyone now knew about, predicting that I wouldn't go to the Eymards but would be the one to put them in their place. In wonder if I wasn't also concerned about defending my hold over Médéric, who I felt was menaced by an obscure and vulgar influence.

It was obvious from the first hours the following Sunday that we were in for very bad weather.

"Nobody but the Eymards are crazy enough to be out on the roads on a day like this," my landlady grumbled. "Oh, I'd like to see that lot get lost, just once!"

I was about to reproach her with being so prejudiced against "that lot" when in the driving snow the most singular vehicle drew up before the door.

"Merciful heavens!" my landlady started in again. "That's the marriage coach Rodrigue Eymard had built in Winnipeg by some famous carpenter there! Nobody's seen it since Maria ran away. That shifty Rodrigue must be up to something if he's taken that thing out. If I was you I'd beware."

"Are you getting superstitious?" I taunted her, laughing, as I hastily buttoned up my coat.

The so-called berline was in reality a sled that sat high above its runners, with a single seat covered by an immense hood of black leather coming down in front to eye level. No sooner had I glimpsed the vehicle through the sheets of drifting snow than I was wild with joy at the idea of confronting the storm from the depths of this flying cavern.

Médéric got out, looking even taller than usual, though I didn't know why until he had taken a few steps toward the door. He was all dressed up in a long, light-coloured overcoat with black frogged buttons and a fur collar to match the fine hat which he wore perched on his forehead. My tramp, whom I had never seen in anything but a buckskin jacket with fringes and cowboy pants, now went so far as to wear gloves. I wanted to smile, despite myself, when a

139

remark from my landlady brought me up short:

"And what's more he's sent the kid dressed up like a man to come and get you!"

In the excitement of the coming drive, I paid little attention to her.

Médéric opened the side door of the sled. The berline was even more attractive inside. A bearskin covered the leather seat and the elegant curve of its back. When I was inside, Médéric covered me with another, softer fur. To keep it dry, he stretched a kind of leather apron attached by snaps to the two arms of the seat. Past the edge of the hood, as if from beneath a visor, you could see out easily and still be well protected. Médéric, having taken his place beside me, gave a low whistle and Gaspard set off.

We were no sooner underway than the powdery snow and buffeting wind came in great gusts from all sides, drawing us into the midst of a delicious dream – we were a longboat borne up on the high waves, a canoe trembling in white water! Médéric and I looked at each other in the half-dark of the berline, our eyes bright with the intense excitement of being exposed together to the angry passion of the earth and sky.

After the clamorous song of the winds, what could be more depressing than the pretentious house where I set foot, greeted by a bulky man in his Sunday best who grew familiar rather quickly and smelled of alcohol a mile away. The idea that Médéric, wild for freedom as I knew him to be, was forced to live in this house put me more than ever on his side.

In the gloomy dining room with heavy furniture and faded velvet hangings, the meal dragged on, served by a woman in sloppy shoes whom the master called by snapping his fingers and sent away as rudely if she lingered a moment to listen, her face tense in the chink of the door.

He was enthroned at the end of the massive table, his stomach contained by an impressive old-fashioned watch-chain, helping himself out of a decanter of wine in front of him. He had tried some twenty times to get Médéric and me to take more than our single glass.

It was only then, after being subjected to so many other surprises, that I noticed Médéric's indoor apparel, which was also new. His suit, with wide chalk stripes on navy-blue and heavily padded shoulders, turned him into a picture out of the city mail-order catalogues, and fitted him as badly as it possibly could. He must have known it from my expression, for suddenly he was embarrassed, as I was at the thought of spoiling his pleasure, even if the suit was in bad taste. In fact, the only one who was quite at ease, especially after a few more glasses of wine, was Rodrigue, who soon launched into an endless monologue.

What was he saying, really? I was paying as little attention as possible to this gloomy room; I had escaped along the path to the hills, which, in the midst of this false decor, seemed to be the only authentic reality. I barely listened to the father's babble about what little chance he'd had to get an education and that was why he was so determined to make his son into a "gentleman," an "elegant fellow," an "educated man . . ."; and all that had so little to do with Médéric, showing no understanding of his real gifts.

All at once I heard myself being addressed:

"Now, they say you're an excellent teacher and you know how to bring the children along. Am I right, or is it a waste of time and money to expect my boy to do well in school? Is he in any way bright?"

I caught Médéric's eye, where in the dark-violet pupil the sign of an old hostility was forming. I answered:

"In a way Médéric is my best pupil. He's the most faithful and the most attached to the things that interest

141

him – nature, for example. . . ."

Rodrigue Eymard pounded his fist on the table.

"Nature, nature! To hell with nature! What I want is education. If Médéric is so bright, why doesn't he give me the satisfaction of being at the top of his class?"

"Maybe because his heart isn't in it."

Rodrigue Eymard exploded into contemptuous and vulgar laughter. At times his whining tone was that of a drunkard trying to get sympathy for his fate. But then I would feel him looking at me with a gaze that was heavy and calculating. He was scrutinizing me with an attention that I could not explain. Surprised by his last change of tone, I now heard him agreeing with me, almost meekly:

"Of course, you have to have your heart in it, but there's heart and heart. You can make some bad mistakes with that heart business.

"That's how I made my big mistake, the biggest one of all. At Médéric's age," he went on, half to himself, "I liked school, and I think I had some talent. God knows what might have happened if I'd had a little guidance from somebody that was thinking about my future."

I was shattered again, for now in that furrowed face with its heavy eyes I fancied I could see the unspeakable suffering of finding at the end of a miscarried life the recollection of a childhood dream. I listened more closely, now taken with pity for this pompous, suffering man.

"That's why," he confided, as if it were in secret, tugging at my sleeve, "that's why I want so much for Médéric to achieve what I never did and suffered because of it." Then he suddenly shouted aloud: "Or I'll break him, I'll break him!"

He calmed down at once and began staring at me again, this time with a kind of affectionate interest that filled me with uneasiness.

"You've got so much influence over him now. He listens

to every word you say. Can't you convince him to settle down and study?''

"I do my best, Monsieur Eymard.''

"Your best?''

The tone, or perhaps the expression on his face, hinted at some unpleasant implication but I had no idea what he was getting at.

"The best the other teachers could do before you, it wasn't much, I'll admit. But you're young and smart and, if I may say so, pretty as a picture. Is your best not irresistible?''

Médéric and I had avoided looking at each other since the father's conversation had taken this dubious turn, but now we couldn't help exchanging a glance, just to make sure that our friendship was not being soiled.

But Rodrigue Eymard changed the subject again, and came back to his obsession of wishing Médéric to accomplish what he himself had been unable to do.

"That wish is very strong, mademoiselle," he said.

And I, still taking him at his word, felt sorry for him once more, but said that he would have more success with Médéric if he let him follow his natural bent, learning in his own way, happy in his own way.

Deep as he was in his cups, Rodrigue, from under his heavy eyelids, shot me a glance of malevolence so pure that I thought he must have grown sober on the spot.

"Happy in his way! Is that the song you sing to him when you go off alone with him in the hills all day?''

I succeeded in controlling myself after this insult, forcing myself to look through the lace curtains at the menacing outdoors. When I had recovered my calm I managed to say:

"The weather's getting worse every minute. I think I should be leaving.''

The master of the house burst out laughing again.

"Why, no, not at all! The real storm won't turn loose for an hour or two yet. We've got time to drink our coffee in the parlour."

When he stood up he was less than sure on his feet and sought the support of my shoulder.

"I'm not in the best of health, mademoiselle, despite appearances. I could leave any day for all we know. Of course, Médéric inherits all this, and my future daughter-in-law, if she's to my taste. You see, I love my boy in my own way, for I've even thought of that."

As we came into the parlour I stopped, astonished, in front of the naïve but fetching portrait of a beautiful young woman. Her eyes were Médéric's, a deep violet full of sad dreams beneath her long, dark lashes.

"My late wife," explained Rodrigue, and burst into one of his loud laughs, whether provoked by unrelieved suffering or tenacious rancour it was hard to tell. "You know, I call her that for convenience sake. She's no more dead than you are, but she might as well be since she left us, me and her precious son. Just think, a woman I took out of her tribe, off the reservation. But she must have been a half-breed already. Look at those eyes – where did she get them if it wasn't from some robber baron? I was under the spell the first time I saw them. I still am, when I see that picture. Those eyes are ridiculous for a boy like Médéric. But in her, they were something different. And can you believe it? Between all the things I could lay at her feet, this house – and it cost a pretty penny – and the expensive furniture, and dresses made in Winnipeg, and the berline signed by the maker, you saw it! and on and on, even servants to look after my Indian, well, between that and the tribe, it was the wigwam, the reservation, she chose."

He jerked his chin contemptuously toward Médéric.

"And him, I wouldn't be surprised if he did the same thing some day. The only hope I have is that you have

144

some influence over him. And you could have more if you wanted and, believe me, mademoiselle, old Eymard knows how to be grateful.''

Leaning on a chair, Médéric fled from his father's voice talking about him as if he weren't there. He was looking away, his face so pale that I was stricken. I compared this moment with the image I had of him on the plateau of the hills, as we gazed down at the endless plain below, when he couldn't resist taking me as witness, very confidentially: ''Mamzelle, from here it's as if we owned the world!''

What hurt most just now was perhaps detecting in Médéric's profile a certain resemblance to his father.

''Mind you, it mightn't do him any harm,'' Rodrigue went on, ''to go and rub shoulders with those little savage girls. They're enticing, know a lot for their age. This young fathead would find he's just about old enough to please them. But if he took my advice, what I'd tell him is, wait for the one that's worth it. Now, in this poor country where the women are brutalized and ignorant, who's worth waiting for if it's not our little schoolteacher, who drops down from heaven, you might say, one fine day. Did I wait for her, my little school mistress, when I was the age of this young fool – maybe a little older! I'd have taken her out, brought her to the dances. . . . But in my day she never came to save me from my ignorance and guide my life.''

His eyes were moist with self-pity.

''My boy's lucky you came,'' he went on. ''That's why I told him, don't miss out with the little teacher. She's your chance, boy.''

I got up and said to Médéric:

''Let's go. Will you bring me home?''

He went out running, came back in the room wearing his coat and carrying mine which he helped me put on.

Rodrigue Eymard, still teetering at the front door, protested that I was leaving far too soon, before we had a chance to get to know each other. His farewell was lost in the gusts of the raging wind.

Though the tempest was now unleashed and we could hear it rushing ahead of us, like water through a broken dam, we didn't suffer its effects too much as long as we remained between the closely planted trees of the lane, which also served to keep us on track in the blinding snow. We sat far apart, each one silent at his end of the seat. From time to time I glanced at Médéric and by the strange reflected light of the flurries saw that his face wore an expression of hurt. At last he murmured in a barely audible voice:

"I'm sorry, mamzelle. I'd never have guessed he'd insult you under our roof. Now I see why he tried to soften me up with all kinds of presents. Oh, he knows the way! You know, mamzelle, my father's a devil!"

I reached out to take his hand and comfort him, but broke off my gesture, realizing I would never dare to complete it, that I must never do so; and from the feeling of that deprivation came a confused regret that seemed to stretch out into an indefinite future, for I wasn't sure who was to be pitied, he or I or any being who, on reaching adulthood, loses a living part of his soul, its spontaneity partially destroyed.

We were reaching the lane's end and would have to confront the full buffeting of the wind, with its deafening tumult that would put an end to all conversation. As we turned out of the lane into the open prairie it was as if we were going from a halfway-navigable tributary into a raging, flooded river in which we had to fight our way upstream. We felt the resistance, the pushing of a wild force that actually became visible on all sides in ghostly shapes, and audible in hysterical, exulting cries. Gaspard

146

was the prow of our frail ship. He ploughed into the tempest, which divided to flow past on either side of the sled with mad velocity, squealing and whistling. At times you would have sworn these were the screams of humans in distress, passing invisible at our sides on drifting rafts.

Médéric, tense with concentration, strove to distinguish the crazy silhouettes invented by the snow and wind from the humble telephone lines that would now be our only guide. He drove as close as he could to the phone line, at the risk of tipping into the ditch. I determined to help him by summoning all my attention to see the next landmark. When it seemed to be long in coming, we feared that we had strayed into the fields and would be lost forever. Then in the surrounding wave, one of us would see a pole and shout to the other. This was how we came to speak to each other again, in snatches, doubtless encouraging one another to stay alive. While, perhaps, we would rather have wished to die.

Soon Médéric would take advantage of the seconds during which a pole could be seen to let Gaspard have a rest, for he was already bathed in sweat. The poor horse would lower his head against the wind in a position of complete exhaustion. A little later he took the initiative of stopping on his own when the landmark appeared, to slump at once in extreme weariness, which made me pity him and must have touched Médéric, though he didn't say a word. In those moments when we waited for Gaspard to rest we could have spoken more easily, but it was precisely then that Médéric seemed most frozen, withdrawn into a silence that made me wonder if he was brooding over his humiliation at having sported his new clothes in an effort to appear older in my eyes, or whether he was suffering from some other, more profound pain.

Suddenly, as if he could hold back no longer, he blurted out:

"I guess . . . I'd better not show up at school anymore after . . . what my dad said. . . ."

Again my hand flew out to take his and stopped halfway. I protested:

"The very opposite, Médéric. You should come now, more than ever! It's your only way out!"

Without replying he urged Gaspard on. Barely rested, the brave creature arched his whole body, lifted his head courageously and struggled to make his way upstream in that impossible current of snow and wind and howls and whistles. Even the berline, which had been such a luxury, now recalled a shipwreck, filled with drifts of snow, like a floundering vessel, the stylish bonnet wobbling and adding to our weight. Médéric said something, and his voice, though close by, seemed strange; whether distorted by the gusts of wind or by emotion, I couldn't tell. He reminded me of what I myself had felt not so very long ago when I found myself cut off from my accustomed habitat, on the verge of adult life. I would have done anything to reassure him: Look, Médéric, it's just a step you have to take. One gets used to it, you'll see . . . But I was not so sure; perhaps this break in one's being, at separation from childhood, left a pain from which one never quite recovered.

It was during those moments when we were both so absorbed by the mystery of our lives that we forgot to keep an eye out for the telephone poles. Suddenly the phone line had disappeared, and apparently the firm earth too, beneath the soft hills of snow. We saw Gaspard plunge into them up to his chest, recover his balance, fall again.

"We're off the road," said Médéric.

He climbed out of the sled and, like Gaspard, went deep into the snow. Bent double under the wind's force, he succeeded in reaching Gaspard and leaning against him. It seemed to me that he put an arm over his neck and perhaps was weeping there, his head against the horse's head. I thought I could discern his shoulders shaking, as when one tries hard to hold back a sob. The horse himself, with little movements of his head, seemed to be trying to console him. I don't know why that scene in the midst of the wind's lament entered my memory forever. A high sheet of flying snow came between us and I lost sight of them, no more than a step or two away. Only the wavy black mane emerged from the white obscurity.

Médéric was approaching along my side of the sled. He put his head inside. I could see his eyes, shining a little through the gusts that swallowed him. And when he spoke, his voice seemed to have crossed years to reach me:

"I think we're lost, mamzelle."

I believe that's exactly what he said. But the tone said, rather: Mamzelle, we're saved. And I trembled, as at good news.

Then Médéric went back to Gaspard. Warm beneath the covers, I gave myself up to the dream of leaving this life. I saw us safe, escaped from evil, from tarnished heredity, from the distortion of the self that one fears perhaps more than anything else in the pride of youth.

Storms were often to wake this same desire in me, but never with the intensity of that first time when I could hear the angels in revolt calling to me through the howling winds. I imagined us, Médéric and I, as they would find us when the storm had passed – two pure statues, hair and lashes powdered with frost, intact and beautiful. Our heads would barely be leaning toward each other.

Back in the sled, Médéric asked, as though he were leaving me the task of deciding for us both:

"What'll we do, mamzelle?"

His docility was infinitely touching.

"What would you do?"

His smile was half sad.

"Cover Gaspard."

"Well, then!"

He took one of our covers and threw it over the horse's back. With his bare hands, into which he blew, he rubbed his neck and tried to warm him, and brushed the snow from his eyes. I felt he was more sorry for Gaspard than for himself and that it was perhaps his horse he was most concerned with saving. And suddenly, as if the white stallion were the first to recover his senses, he started off again, hauling the berline with a great tug from the soft snow where it had sunk so deep. Médéric leapt aboard as the sled passed. He let the reins go slack, and soon remarked:

"We're back on the road."

"How can you tell?"

"The way he walks. Can't you feel it? He's more sure of himself. Good horse, he's got more sense than lots of people."

Just then the slim silhouette of a telephone pole slid vaguely past in the storm. And we started to laugh; the incredible insouciance of our age was given back to us.

"You were scared," Médéric teased.

"Not at all," I told him. "I didn't think we were really lost."

"Oh, yes, you thought so all right."

We had slipped back into the tone of friendly familiarity. I noticed it and isolated myself in silence. Shortly after, a thin black line appeared feebly between sky and earth.

"Beauchamp's woods," Médéric said. "We'll be right beside it for about a mile. Then there's a stretch of open road but it's uphill and the snow doesn't drift there."

He concluded, as if he were making fun of the idea:

"So, I guess we're safe and sound."

Why then was I so melancholy deep within me? It occurred to me that we might live long, Médéric and I, that we might grow old. The thought was really too impossible. I thrust it from me. I leaned back in the seat, out of the wind, as Médéric had said he could now find the line of trees by himself, and that I should sleep if I felt tired.

I closed my eyes, but not from need of sleep. It was so

150

that I could dream at ease. The notion of dying, or even of growing old, had left me, and I took the fancy of imagining myself going through life without ever changing my age. I would travel, travel a lot, I thought, encouraged in this feeling by the rocking of the berline, which was less rough now, more regular. I would visit far countries, cities, incomparable places. I saw myself reaching a high future from which I would look back with some commiseration toward the awkward little country teacher I had been.

I opened my eyes. I found myself looking into one of the two four-sided lanterns, their glass prettily set in lead, which made a pair on either side of the sleigh. The darkened glass sent back a reflection of my face. It seemed to me vague, graceful, with distant eyes that pierced the whirling snow, and stray locks of hair that foamed and glistened. . . . I couldn't look away.

Suddenly, beside my own face appeared that of Médéric who had come closer without knowing that the glass reflected him as well. He leaned toward me, perhaps to see if I was sleeping. As I neither moved nor spoke he may have thought I was dozing. My eyes half closed, I watched him in the mirror of the lantern where, borne on drifting snow, our two faces passed, blurred like an old wedding photo. Then the snow cleared and I saw that Médéric's face was turned toward mine. A lock of hair, fluffed and wild, escaped from my bonnet and rose up and touched his face. Motionless, staring at the lantern glass, I saw him take off his glove and try to catch the stray lock. He almost caught it in mid-air but stopped, his hand in suspense, surprised at himself and at his gesture. His look was one of infinite astonishment and a tenderness that one never sees again in love once satisfied, nor even once it knows that it is love. He seemed at the same time to be floating on islets of snow, and I had the curious impression that everything I saw was happening only in the lantern, which had invented a game in which neither Médéric nor I was

151

really taking part. But then it showed me his face again, distorted, then closing his eyes in the first fright of the heart as it came to him.

I promptly put back the stray lock under my wool bonnet. I leaned back as far as possible to my end of the seat, thus losing sight of the lantern with its troubling visions.

I spoke lightly:

"We're through the worst, aren't we? Pretty soon we'll see the village and the school, all the things that bother you, poor Médéric!"

He was recovering slowly from the embarrassment that had surprised him, but his gaze was still half captive and confused.

"As far as school goes, I'm not sure it'll see me anymore," he muttered. "Or the village, for that matter."

"And where are you going to spend your life?"

I was trying to tease him and bring him back to what I supposed to be his normal self. The storm was less violent now. Despite the poor visibility we no longer had to expose our heads by constantly sticking them out, but left everything to Gaspard who was trotting firmly along, sure of the now-familiar road. A hand's breadth away the wind, still high-mettled, rushed by, shaking at the bonnet but no longer really threatening. Now our progress was merely a feeling of elation. I took extreme pleasure in it, comparing it to life flying by. Yes, that was how life now appeared to me – a long, triumphant race in a state of ever-renewed elation. I had forgotten the unhappy afternoon I had just escaped.

I said to Médéric, carried away by the joy of our drive:

"In this berline, with you and Gaspard, I could go to the ends of the earth."

He got in the spirit of the game, liberated by my return of gaiety.

"Shall we go? To Manitou! To La Rivière!"

These were villages forty, fifty miles away.

I went him one better:

"Swan Lake! Mariapolis!"

He followed up:

"New York! Philadelphia!"

Our resolve to flee pleased me so much that when I saw a feeble light blinking through the blowing snow, I cried sadly:

"Oh, no! We're coming to the village! What a pity! I'd gladly go the whole way again for the fun of being so warm in your berline in the middle of the winds from nowhere!"

I hadn't finished my sentence when, standing up, Médéric was forcing Gaspard to turn around.

This time my hand flew to Médéric's arm, to stop him at once.

"Come on! Do you think I'd have the heart to send Gaspard back and back again?"

"Ah," he said, turning Gaspard back to the path, "he'd have done it, mamzelle!" – and all his sadness returned.

We had suddenly fallen from our wild elation. I saw again the pompous dining room, the heavy furniture, the stiff drapes, and Rodrigue Eymard, the unbalanced man with the beady eyes, spying on us, his son and me.

In a moment we were in front of the house where I stayed. Gaspard stopped of his own accord but Médéric remained stock-still, his eyes lowered, as if concentrating on a frightful thought.

"Here we are, Médéric!"

He looked up, astonished, hastened to open the little door and came with me to the house. I invited him in to get warm. But my landlady's step was approaching, and he began to back away, embarrassed, saying he didn't like that woman, nor anybody in the village . . . and better he should go before Gaspard got too chilled.

When my landlady arrived she found me alone on the doorstep in the midst of the storm, and she had a little smile on her face that spoke volumes.

153

Things were never the same again between Médéric and me. Though he had passed fourteen some time ago he continued to come to school. But why did he bother? He paid less and less attention all the time. He had found a warm stable on the edge of the village with a stall for Gaspard. He went there each noon hour to look after him and, in the moist half-dark, share with him his apple and sandwiches. He had never really made friends in the school, as he was older than most of the others; but now he kept apart from everyone and had no companion but his horse. When he came back from tending it he brought an aura of stable smell, and one day I couldn't help mentioning the fact. He gave me a reproachful look but didn't say anything to excuse himself.

That wasn't the only thing that grated on my nerves. He now wore the hateful new suit with chalk stripes that I had seen for the first time the Sunday I had dined with Rodrigue. In that suit he gave the impression of a tall young man who had wandered into school by mistake and stayed on among my little ones for no good reason. Trying to make my point in a light-hearted way, I told him once that I thought his usual clothes suited him better than this flashy suit, which was much too old for him. But it was no use; he went on wearing it, perhaps to defy me and perhaps because nothing mattered to him anymore.

It's true that during those few weeks it seemed I had something to find fault with almost every day – either I was getting nervous or he was growing more impossible. I had, in fact, just ticked him off for wearing clothes too old for him when, seeing his legs stretched into the aisle for his silly game of tripping little girls, I got angry and told him it was ridiculous for a boy of his age to indulge in such childishness. This time he took my stare with a slightly smart-aleck expression that also had a touch of regret, as if he was sorry for me, seeing me so changeable. Most of the time, however, he was lost in morose daydreams. His

154

homework was hopeless. He would sit for hours in a kind of sad inertia, reminiscent of a traveller lost in a plain without landmarks, not knowing which way to go, unable to decide to move. Then my heart would go out to him as it had in the best days, and I tried with all my strength to remind him of the feeling he had had for nature, recalling things he had liked so much that he made me like them too. He did no more than give a sad smile, as if to say that this kind of happiness was lost to him.

One day, as he was reciting his lesson aloud, his voice changed so abruptly that everyone looked around to find the stranger. The little girls were the first to realize that this was Médéric's voice. A few of them burst out laughing, pretending to hide their faces in their hands. Médéric, in his embarrassment, looked almost surly. He refused to read aloud again. He would read in a low mumble that I could hardly hear from my desk – I no longer went to sit by him at the other end of the bench, and I never asked him to come to my desk.

Thus I came to hold him at a distance precisely at the time when he needed help the most, because it bothered me to see him shooting up so quickly before my very eyes. He was still growing and his face had become extremely thin. It looked like a greyhound's, all forehead, the eyes high-set, gazing sadly around at everything.

After class one evening he offered to help tidy up. I used to ask the older ones to give a hand, but had exempted Médéric because he lived too far away and the least delay would have meant his arriving home near nightfall. But now the days were growing longer.

"Very well," I said, "stay if you like, it's certainly your turn."

Then Médéric, who had hated doing the slightest thing that smacked of domestic work – even bringing a pail of water – started sweeping the floor almost joyously. As I sat at my desk correcting compositions I could hear him come and go, moving the benches to sweep underneath,

155

not too worried, it's true, about dislodging all the dust, but with such an evident desire to please that my heart was suddenly softened. I suspected that he wanted to speak to me alone, that this was why he had offered to clean up but didn't know how to start. I decided to help him along. Pencil in hand, appearing only half available to chat, I asked him, trying not to sound too serious:

"Are things going better with your father now?"

The burden of his hesitation seemed to lift. He came forward.

"Oh, mamzelle, he's really sorry for what happened that time you came. You know, he doesn't often drink that much. He says it was the emotion at having somebody young in the house and if you ever came back it wouldn't be like the other time. You must have a bad memory of that. He says he'd give the world to wipe it all out with another dinner one of these days, if you'd agree."

"But I thought that was a closed book, Médéric."

He looked down.

"If you don't want to come back to our place my father says I can have the berline to take you any place you want to go, 'cause you liked it so much."

"But where on earth would we go, Médéric?"

"Oh," he murmured in some embarrassment, not looking at me, "we could go to the next village. There's a movie theatre and all kinds of things to do. My father thinks you must be bored, a young girl all alone in this place and nobody to take you out."

I was flabbergasted. Médéric, so haughty and contemptuous a short time before, was almost begging me, and – what made it worse – with a broom in his hands.

I told him he had done enough and I would finish cleaning. I glanced up to meet his eyes and found his natural pride struggling against an obscure impulse to submission, which both made me sorry for him and turned me against him.

I tried to be as schoolmarmish as possible:

156

"I'm not at all bored by my work, Médéric. It's my whole life. The only passion I have. It's quite enough for me."

He had the courage to reply:

"But you were so happy sledding in the snow. We were free! You said you'd like to go back and do the trip all over again in the storm!"

I turned to him:

"I hope you haven't gone and told that to anybody?"

He bowed his head in admission.

Now he seemed so discouraged at having displeased me that I had to force myself to reassure him.

"Oh, well, that's not so important. But, Médéric, I don't want to judge your father. He's suffered a lot. Still, don't listen to everything he says."

"Who should I listen to, then?"

What was I to say?

"To yourself."

His strange eyes with their sunset violet stared at me pathetically, as though silently calling for help.

"You don't like me anymore, mamzelle."

I looked long at him and realized that Médéric, unaware of his own feelings, meant that I didn't pay as much attention to him in class as I had before.

I smiled at him in a friendly way.

"Oh, Médéric, of course I do. There's not another pupil that I worry about as much, if you want to know. If you did well I'd be the happiest teacher in the world. But you're lazy, you're a do-nothing, and that makes me unhappy."

His reproach was sorrowful:

"But you'd never come with me up to the hills again, or even on the road in the berline."

"No, Médéric, that's all finished for me. Anyway, I don't have time. From now on I'm going to give all my time to my class. If you want to please me, do the same."

I pretended to go back to my work. Stuck there in front

157

of me, he hesitated for a long moment, then, with a vestige of his old bravado, laid his broom across the scattered papers on my desk, shrugged his independence and wandered back to his desk, whistling. Yet a sagging of his thin frame betrayed so touching a vulnerability that I was saddened. I said to myself that I was treating him with undue severity because he was so tall and I was young, punishing him, in a way, for my own indiscretion.

At his desk he was feverishly gathering up his books and scribblers, even his dictionary – he was the only one in the school to own such a thing. I thought: He's testing me, he's showing off; I mustn't seem to take it seriously. And I put on an air of indifference, though my heart was beating with distress. Because, suddenly, at the idea of losing him, he became precious beyond what I could ever have imagined. His bundle made and held by a leather strap, he took one step in the aisle and stared into my eyes with his strange look of exhaustion and deep solitude.

"Mamzelle, I don't know what I'm doing in school anymore. I don't see why I should come back."

Protests rose in my heart, a thousand kind words to hold him back. Too young, too clumsy, perhaps too vexed, I could answer nothing but:

"If it's only to learn nothing, if you don't want an education, then I really don't see why . . ."

I had no time to say more. In a recurrence of his old violence he turned on his heel and left with long strides, his school things dragging at the strap's end, like a ball on a chain from which he was about to free himself forever.

Who could have convinced me a few months earlier that, once rid of my most difficult pupil, my class would become boredom itself to me? A dozen times a day I caught myself looking toward the empty bench. And toward the snow-covered plain where so often the flying black mane, the only thing visible against the expanse of white, had warned me of the boy's approach at full gallop. And I had felt the thrill of a pleasure comparable, I suppose, to that experienced when we have tamed an animal and see it come at our call.

He'll come back after the big March storms – they're often the worst of the year . . . I thought, and then, after all this rain is over and the mud dries . . . As if wind and rain or mud and storms would ever have stopped Médéric from going where he pleased.

I could imagine him wandering around the dark, gloomy house, or perhaps poring over a volume of the encyclopedia; or idle, neglected, exposed only to his father's influence, which I suspected might well be exerted to detach him from me, after having tried the very opposite. . . . Would that be the determining influence, after all? Or that of his mother and the primitive innocence he had partly inherited from her? – though perhaps that was his greatest misfortune, for it left him so disarmed against the world's deceptions that he barely had a chance from the very start. Or would I win out in the end? Sometimes I thought it would still be possible. Then I would find myself watching the distant plain with such a wish to see the young rider appear that I actually imagined he was there. And would realize that what I had taken for horse and rider was no more than a play of light and clouds, or the wind moving over the prairie.

Springtime arrived. It was born, you might say, at sunrise one fine day. For weeks it had been covertly preparing its coming under heavy clouds, grey skies and driving rain, and now, on the first sunny day, we saw it open before our eyes.

I had never before seen the birth of springtime on the prairies. A more delicate birth you cannot imagine. There is nothing here to announce its coming, no ice jams or

breakups, no crashing of ice in liberated waters such as I
had known in my native city. Nothing but discreet, small
voices, wet under last year's grass and in shallow ditches.
Waters run softly there, for there's scarcely any slope; but
in the silent space that gathers them, rejoicing in them,
these thin, liquid songs have more effect than any noisy,
swollen river.

On the earth, bare of snow at last, black from one
horizon to the other, appeared the tenuous threads of
young green shoots tracing a barely visible seam of harvest
yet to come. A bird sang somewhere in the immensity,
suspending all other sounds. Its song seemed to come from
everywhere at once in the open land, and you would have
been hard put to find its source by looking. Sometimes you
would find the singer just over your head on the telegraph
wires, seeming to make fun of you for having sought him
throughout the sky.

This delicate spring, this graceful spring, revived my
regrets. I was inconsolable over my failure with Médéric. It
seemed to matter little that my class was docile and loving,
that almost all the parents were now satisfied with me. My
smallest pupils devoured me with their eyes all shining with
love and I, like a fool, possessed by a conviction of failure,
paid little attention to their gift, although it still has no
equal for me in the world. Such was the power of the
obsession that was mine during those teaching years; and I
now know that of all those that capture us totally, to make
or break us, this one is as exacting and dominating as any.

But I had almost stopped expecting anything when, leaning on the window-sill one day, I saw in the distance the
black, flying mane of the white horse. They were not coming on at a gallop this time, but rather slowly, as if unwill-
ingly, only half resigned to their return. Médéric leapt
down from Gaspard, tied him to the flagpole and loped
toward the school. When I saw that he had his books under
his arm I trembled a little in triumph. But I went back to

160

my desk, determined to greet him with signs of pleasure that would be tempered by a teacher's dignity. Nonetheless, my heart beat faster.

So my tactics had succeeded, Médéric was back; and if something good came of it for his life it would be partly due to my efforts. In that moment I understood how well the parable of the sheep lost and found again could apply to a school class, and I gave up rebelling against my feeling that there was more joy in his return than in the docile flock.

Médéric's shadow crossed the door-sill before him, and then he stood there, a lanky, young man-child with the haunted look of someone who has been lost for days and days. It seemed to me that he was at the end of his rope and had come here because he didn't know where else to go. The upper part of his face – his eyes veiled with their long lashes – was that of Médéric as I remembered him. But the lines of his mouth, those thick lips – or was it the shadow above his upper lip? – changed his physiognomy completely. This lower part now showed a certain resemblance to Rodrigue Eymard; while his eyes, soft, sad and lost in a distant reverie, preserved the candour that came perhaps from his mother. I had never yet seen so clearly the transitory linkage between child and man, which lasts until the one takes over; and they appeared so ill-assorted, I remember feeling sorry for both.

Médéric had no greeting for either me or his companions. He slid along the aisle and flopped down at his desk, having trouble to fit his long legs underneath. I wanted to find a kind word of greeting for him, but was too stupefied by the change in him and couldn't open my mouth. I tried to go on with my class as if nothing had happened, to give him time to get his bearings. At one moment, going down the aisle past his desk I stopped and asked him to try and follow the lesson. He opened his book submissively at the proper page, but that was as far as it

161

went. He seemed unable to steer his mind. It didn't appear to be his former voyages that now carried off his imagination. It was turning, turning in circles around itself, its own hitching post.

The day dragged on miserably. Yet everything outside was like a soft caress. That morning on the way to school I had already noticed how the air had the purity of a child's breath. The signs of renewing life were everywhere. One of the children had brought me a bouquet of pussy willows; they never failed to touch me, no doubt because this young vegetable life is so close to that of a tiny animal in its first days. Wouldn't you think, as you touch them, that you're patting some little creature sound asleep in its silken down! Another child had brought me the year's first crocus, plucked by the roadside at the edge of a melting drift of snow.

We would have been happy together if it hadn't been for the presence of this young stranger whose mouth was shaped in a man's bitterness. Why is it that the appearance of the man in the child is a painful sight, whereas the loveliest thing in the world is the fleeting rediscovery of the child in a man?

To my surprise, when the day was over and the other children gone, Médéric stayed at his place, apparently wanting to speak to me but so embarrassed that nothing would come out. Only his eyes spoke, gloomy and sad, as if to interpret to me some complaint of his spirit or some vague accusation.

As the silence between us grew unbearable, I asked:
"What's wrong, Médéric?"

His lip began to tremble. I thought for a moment that this simple question was going to bring tears, and I had never seen him near to crying. With this uncontrollable emotion the child showed so clearly through his young man's get-up that I went to sit beside him at his desk as I had done not so long ago, and he showed his pleasure by giving me the beginnings of a smile. But then I didn't know

162

what to say and we were silent for a long time, staring straight ahead in the empty classroom, and I remember thinking that we were like two travellers in the same seat of a train that refuses to leave the station.

I looked up front to the lessons I had written on the board or the drawings I had done, feeling slightly wrong and absent-minded because I didn't know what to do about this too-tall adolescent beside me who, I realized, was so moved that he was trembling slightly. Finally I looked at him, and in his eyes, fixed on mine, I saw the astonishment, the wonder, and the suffering of a first love which, in its budding stage, does not yet know itself by name and trembles with fear and joy and misunderstood desire. If I hadn't just been through it myself, could I have known what Médéric was suffering from, and would I have tried so hard to distract him, so that he would be spared of seeing more clearly into his torment and confusion? But I didn't succeed in turning him away from the desperate search within himself for something stable, certain, customary, for everything in him at that moment went beyond the state of his knowledge.

At last, as if he could no longer bear to be led into the unknown, not understanding what was happening to him, Médéric let his head fall gently to my shoulder. And it made me sad to realize that his infinite loneliness drove him to me for help, just when I should have kept him at a distance to avoid hurting him more. Yet I could not make up my mind to waken him from the gentle torpor into which he had fallen as he leaned against me. His head, despite his thick, abundant hair, was light on my shoulder. His face was pale. His hands lay inert on his knees. Suddenly he raised them to his heart, as if the hurt, the surprise to his flesh, had touched him there.

He groaned weakly:

"Oh, mamzelle! What's happening to me? It's as if I was in . . ."

He was stifling with embarrassment.

163

"It's not my fault. I didn't do it on purpose."

I dared a very small caress, smoothing the dark hair back on the side of his head.

"Médéric, nobody ever did it on purpose, nobody!"

Before he could become too conscious of the state of things, I took his head in my hands and laid it gently against the back of the bench. I got up and returned to my desk. A fly that the spring warmth had awakened from its winter torpor was butting against everything with a hard sound that tortured my nerves. I could have groaned as well at the sight of Médéric, his eyes closed, barely breathing. I felt that I was spectator to the death of a child under pressure from the man to whom he was giving birth. I thought I should go to the rescue of that part of Médéric that was threatened, whatever the cost; but I didn't know how to start, I didn't know what to do.

He half opened his eyes. He saw me at my desk, hiding behind my job, the books and scribblers forming a wall between us. Two tears glistened, held back by thick lashes. Then, clumsily, Médéric began collecting his school things, not angry or hasty this time but rather against his own will. He stopped a few times to look at the walls, the pictures, the row of encyclopedias on a shelf, the big map of the two continents: North America, South America. Then he was standing in the aisle, not knowing how to say good-bye.

"It was a good time for me," he began politely and with just the right distance – but suddenly his voice broke.

"Why do you talk like that, Médéric? What's to stop you from coming back? You'll always have your place here."

He wagged his head sadly, a sign that in a way he had lost that place through his own fault though not on purpose.

"But good heavens, Médéric, what's going to become of you?"

He shrugged, indifferent.

164

"What does it matter?"

"Come now, Médéric!"

He turned toward me, his eyes suddenly darkening.

"What's it to you, after all?"

After a long moment I murmured at his back, which was retreating:

"Very well, depending on what becomes of you, it's a great sorrow or a great joy. That's it. I can't be indifferent to what happens."

Slowly he turned toward me again, then, finding nothing to say, continued on his way with his gliding step. I pursued him with a reproach which I thought might still reach him.

"You say you think a lot of me, but that doesn't even inspire you to try and live up to my hopes for you."

This time he turned violently, and there was a good deal of Rodrigue Eymard in his jutting jaw.

"What more do you want, anyway?"

I gave him time to calm down, waited a moment and said, as if to myself:

"I'd like to find again, before you leave school, if you have to leave – I'd like to find my companion of the hills. Will I ever see him again, Médéric?"

He looked up, showing eyes overflowing with pain and mixed with resentment as well as tenderness which he couldn't succeed in hiding.

Then he fled from the school at a run, like a frightened child.

The end of the school year came swiftly, unexpectedly. Médéric had still not appeared since that feverish first day of spring that had awakened him to the needs of nature. I was deeply sorry for him, but found it wise that he should stay away. Yet I wanted nothing so much as to see him again before my departure. I

165

had been offered a post at a school in town and was to leave for good at the end of June. We were going to have a classroom party to mark my departure and the end of the term. Surely, I thought, Médéric will hear about it and come to say good-bye.

I was pleased with the idea of my new post, which I had obtained in spite of my youth, yet I was aware that I was leaving behind an experience that would be unique in my life. Never again would I be likely to know the deep exultation of involvement that had bound me to this village on the threshold of virgin land. I had before me a world of discoveries; but I realized that behind me there already lay things that were forever lost, and that if life gives with one hand it can take away with the other. Thus my feeling of triumph was somewhat tarnished. For the first time I was aware that in order to advance one step, one must tear oneself away from some possession perhaps even more precious.

The party took place, and was simple and touching. The children had decorated the school with leaves and flowers. The parents sent cakes and delicacies. One mother arrived with an enormous basket of cups and saucers, another brought a pitcher of coffee wrapped in thick towels to keep it hot. The school board was represented. The village blacksmith, who was the head trustee, wringing his hammer-hardened hands, made a speech which he may have prepared but which came out as if just freshly composed. He said that their poor, isolated village had had more than its share of older teachers, who had their good points but were often too strict or perhaps already tired; and that for once to see a "young thing" here was reason to be grateful, because youth almost always left behind a spark of life.

I listened to him, chilled and distressed, thinking more of my countless blunders than of the spark I was supposed to have communicated to each pupil. My children let

166

themselves go so far as to speak more directly from the heart. A little girl, in a burst of feeling, came to throw her arms around my neck, weeping: "Now you're leaving, what's going to become of us?"

"Come, come," I said, holding her close, "there'll be another young lady next year, and you may like her even more than me!"

"Oh," she wailed, as if I had profaned the feeling of exclusivity that is a part of every love, "what a thing to say!"

Of course it was gratifying to leave regret and sorrow behind me. Nowhere else did I ever leave behind so much. It was as if this place in the world was to be that of the most touching solidarity for me. As I leaned down to kiss the little girl who was crying, I must have recognized that through her I was consoling myself for not having the other child to console.

All day, even at the times when I was least alone, perhaps precisely at those times, I watched across the plain for the distant apparition of a young rider galloping toward the school. So as not to blame Médéric I told myself that his father had no doubt kept him home, trying to turn him against me.

The time came to separate for good from these children whom I had held as close to my heart as if they had been my own. But what am I saying! They were mine, and would be mine even when I had forgotten their names and faces, remaining a part of me as I would a part of them, by virtue of the most mysterious possessive force in existence, one that sometimes even surpasses the bond of blood. Was my life to consist then of such violent separations, or would it finally lead to an enduring attachment?

I hugged them, large and small, and even some of the parents who were carried away by the emotion of the occasion. One mother, after thanking me for the progress her children had made, congratulated me on having been able "so cleverly to get rid of" Médéric Eymard before he

could turn into the "bad apple that rots the whole barrel."
I stared at her with such disapproval that she in turn began
to stare at me suspiciously, ready to take back, if she had
been able, the compliments just made. And that was really
the only thing said about Médéric that day. He might have
been buried alive in that oblivion.

I was alone. For the last time I sat down at my desk. I
contemplated the walls, the pictures, Médéric's bench and,
through the windows, the endless distance. Then I left the
place. I locked up my little village school. On the way past
I left the key with the secretary of the school board. He
saw the tears in my eyes, and you'd have thought he was
offended:

"Are you crazy, getting sad over a dump like this when
you have the luck to be going to a good job in town,
among civilized people? Another year or two with us and
you'd have started to be like us. Keenness and fire are not
lasting things. Life snuffs them out the way you bury a
prairie fire."

Was that all I'd been – a prairie fire?

The next day some of the children were at the station to
see me off. This was a comfort but also an affliction, for I
saw at first glance that Médéric was not among them. I
leaned out of the train as it began to move off. I saw the
fragile forms, so tiny against the sky in those parts, making
enormous gestures, as they would to someone sailing away
from shore. And on the wharf of the infinite, the frail
children dwindled before my eyes. I felt I was abandoning
them; and that those silent, overwhelming, dismal spaces
in all their vastness were closing around them, cutting me
off from my poor, deserted children.

I suppose one has to have been a school mistress in one
of those half-dead villages of the prairie to understand
what I felt – the heady certainty of having left in their lives
a memory that nothing could erase, but also the heartbreak
of leaving them, the knot of remorse so tight that it seemed

168

impossible it could ever be loosened to let me breathe. Watching these small silhouettes, already indistinct, I was thinking about another child, perhaps motionless on the prairie somewhere, on a hillock from which he could watch the train carrying me off and be glad of it.

Almost as soon as it had gathered speed, the train reached the edge of the village and stopped. Here a short lateral line built for the benefit of the next village joined the main railway. The trainman climbed down, took from a tool-shed a steel bar with a flattened tip, used it to open the switch and replaced his bar. He climbed aboard and we were on our way again, backing along the secondary line toward the neighbouring village which had never forgiven the CNR for sending its trains in tail-first, considering the affront so serious that it had drawn up petition after petition in order to have its train come in head-first like everybody else's. Sitting in this reverse train on its way to an angry village, I had laughed to myself, sometimes out loud; but today I couldn't muster a smile.

We stopped there only three or four minutes, just time enough to pick up one passenger and a few parcels, and started back for the main line, this time head-first. I could now look only with a detached eye at the passing flatness of the countryside, attractive as it was with its innumerable tiny flowers of every colour which, toward the end of June, turn this ordinary landscape into one of the most delicately coloured in the world. My thoughts were elsewhere. Suddenly I was reminded that the dirt road parallel to the tracks was the one along which Médéric and I had driven in the berline through the raging storm. Today it was a very quiet road, but in my mind there remained the whistling winds and the emotions of that impetuous night. I thought again of Médéric, reflected in the lantern glass that evening, his face turned toward me, astonished, full of wonder. Shaken by the train, this image ran ahead of me, over the canvas of humble flowers scattered through the fields of young wheat or oats. And though it had never been my intention to encourage Médéric's budding love, I knew at this moment that I would be sorry to think it dead. What did I really want except to be adored from afar like a star guiding him through life? – child that I was myself!

At last we were back at the junction of the lines. The trainman climbed down again and took his bar from the toolshed. It was then, as I looked out for a last glimpse of the place, that I saw, coming at breakneck speed from the distant plain, Médéric, almost lying forward on the horse, his big hat thrown back and dancing on his shoulders. Dressed exactly as on the first day I had seen him, on his white horse with its wavy black mane, and the vast country empty all around him, he left graven on my mind a picture almost identical to that of his arrival at the school: my last view of Médéric.

The trainman had closed the switch. He put away his bar and locked the toolshed. He gave the departure signal to the engineer, who was leaning out the locomotive window taking the air. The trainman jumped aboard and the little convoy was underway. Médéric was coming along. I urged him on in my imagination, desperate for him to catch up. Then I saw him cut across at a point where the train curved. On the pommel I thought I could make out some object that he was protecting with one hand, and I believed, I don't know why, that it was for me.

When the train had rounded the curve Médéric was already waiting for us on top of a little rise. Behind him was an immensity of firmament such as I have never seen again. Médéric was searching desperately for me in the train. In those days when we travelled by rail in summer, we left the windows wide open. Médéric had been quick to find me as I half leaned out. High in the air he raised what his hand was holding, whirled it two or three times for impetus, then with great accuracy hurled it through the window onto my lap. It was an enormous bouquet of field

170

flowers, light as a butterfly, barely holding together its fragile stems with their awkward grace; yet it reached me without flying apart, loosening a little to show me its corollas still fresh with dew.

I had never seen at one time so many different wild flowers of that countryside. No doubt there were some from the fields nearby, but there were others that must have come from unsuspected hiding places, such as these rein-orchids from the creekside that needed shade the summer long. I imagined Médéric searching the underbrush since dawn, searching dry earth, wet earth, right to the first slopes of the hills, so that not the smallest flower of this tender season would be missing from his offering.

Our eyes met. Under his battered hat his face seemed attentive, serious and loving, as on the day - a century ago! - when the trout in the icy water had let themselves be caressed and he asked: "There's mystery everywhere, don't you think?"

Silently my lips formed the only words that came to my heart: Oh, Médéric, Médéric!

He raised his hand high, high in the bright sky, with a gesture that seemed to be for now and forever. Gaspard saluted in his own way with two great, impatient tosses of his head. The next curve in the line hid them from my view.

I stared at the bouquet resting in my lap, a simple strand of grass tied around it like a ribbon. It gave off a delicate odour. It spoke of the young and fragile summer, barely born but it begins to die.

ABOUT THE AUTHOR

Gabrielle Roy's prominent role in the literature of Canada was established with the publication of her first novel in 1945. That book, *The Tin Flute* (or *Bonheur d'occasion*, as it was titled in the original French), was awarded the Prix Fémina, thus becoming the first Canadian work to win a major French literary prize. It also earned a Governor-General's Award, plus medals from the Académie Française and the Académie Canadienne Française. In 1947 Miss Roy was elected to the Royal Society of Canada, and in 1967 she was made a Companion of the Order of Canada. She won a second Governor-General's Award in 1957, this time for *Street of Riches*, which also won the Prix Duvernay. In 1971 the Quebec government awarded her the Prix David for her entire body of work.

Upon publication in Quebec, *Children of My Heart* earned the author her third Governor-General's Award in 1978. In the same year she received the Molson prize for her entire body of work.

Other books by Gabrielle Roy available in English are *Where Nests the Water Hen, The Cashier, The Hidden Mountain, The Road Past Altamont, Windflower, Enchanted Summer* and *Garden in the Wind*.

DATE DUE
DATE DE RETOUR

MAR 2 8 1992	JAN 0 9 2006	
Apr 1/2:25pm		
FEB 1 6 1993		
VF.		
MAY 1 5 1998		
MAR 0 4 1998		
MAR 10 6:40pm		
NOV 1 8 1998		
DEC 1 1 1998		
FEB 0 1 1999		
JAN 2 7 1999		
MAY 1 5 2000		
FEB 0 1 2000		
NOV 2 0 2002		
DEC 1 2 2002		
DEC 1 2 2002		
JAN 1 5 2004		